ERSATZ WINES

Other Books by Christopher Priest

Novels:

The Separation
The Extremes
The Prestige
The Quiet Woman
The Glamour
The Affirmation
A Dream of Wessex
The Space Machine
Inverted World
Fugue For a Darkening Island
Indoctrinaire

Short story collections:

Real-Time World
An Infinite Summer
The Dream Archipelago

Non-fiction

The Magic - the story of a film

Ersatz Wines

Christopher Priest

To Tim

Very best wishes

Christopher Priest

GrimGrin
Studio

To Charles Platt

This book was first published in 2008 by:
GrimGrin Studio
32 Elphinstone Road
Hastings, East Sussex, TN34 2EQ
United Kingdom
grimgrin@gmx.com

ISBN: 978-0-9559735-4-3 (hardback)

Printed by Lightning Source

Contents

Introduction

i

This is a book about a writer's beginnings, about in fact my own beginnings. With a few digressions before and after it describes a short period of my life in the 1960s when the only thing that interested me, indeed obsessed me, was the wish to become a writer. I say 'short period', because that is how it seems now, so many years later, but at the time it felt like a long grind with not much hope of ending or success.

To become a writer is a fairly common ambition – in a survey of 2,461 people of working age in Britain in 2007, almost a tenth said that they wanted to become an author. The success of book groups and writers' circles also underlines what a persistent aspiration it is for many people. In the USA alone, more than twenty million people belong to writers' groups or are registered for creative writing courses. Most of these people will inevitably not achieve their dream, although in these days of internet publishing and print-on-demand books, many more will do so than perhaps were able to in the past.

Even though so many people are doing it, at the beginning most writers are isolated from each other and often find it difficult to make contact with others on the same wavelength. In isolation, they have little with which to compare themselves. This was my case. I was full of doubts not only about my ability, but also about my general suitability for the job. For a while I sought enlightenment in literary biographies and autobiographies, hoping for some clue about how to proceed, a way of short-cutting the long slow process of learning, rejection and dashed hopes.

I discovered that not only were most writers' lives different from each other, so that no helpful-seeming pattern emerged, but they were noticeably different from my own. I felt these successful writers all seemed to spring from backgrounds where there was a constant strain of adventure or strangeness or exotica or character-forming hardship. I was different. I had not been educated as a homesick boarder in one of Britain's great public schools, subject to fagging and flogging and nocturnal experiences in the dorm. Nor had I suffered privation and malnutrition in the slums. I had not endured war. I had not travelled the world. I was not an émigré. I had been neither a success nor a failure. While neglecting to traumatize me by being neither rich nor poor, my parents had not provided me with any literary antecedents. I had not been a pilot in the RAF, I was not a lapsed Catholic, a famous Lothario, an alcoholic, a criminal, a master spy, a round-the-world sailor, a mountaineer ... I had not been a teacher or a publisher or a television actor or *anything* that had even a remote link to the world of books.

It seemed there were a lot of things I had been not. Instead I had been born and brought up in a quiet suburb in the south of Manchester. My father went to work in an office every day, my mother stayed at home and brought up me and my two sisters. I went to the local grammar school, and when I left I – well, that's for later.

So my writing career began unpromisingly, from cold, not long after I left school, when I was at the end of my teens. By the time I was twenty-five, though, I had written and sold my first novel to publishers in Britain and the USA, and I was just about able to support myself financially by writing full-time. I had no special advantages that I'm aware of. I was simply someone who wanted to write, to get what I had written published and eventually to live the life of a writer. It wasn't easy, and the outcome was never guaranteed, but in the end it turned out to be achievable.

I've put this book together with the intention of showing as straightforwardly as possible what I did and what I wrote. Like most established writers I am often asked about how I got started, what I had to do to 'break into print', and so on. This is the fullest possible answer to that enquiry.

I view the stories here as instructive, but not instructional. There are no lessons, just the sight of a young, untutored writer setting about his business and discovering what he could or could not do, and perhaps what he should and should not write. Progress is made. Each succeeding story reveals lessons have been learned. This is the point. I have always maintained that writing cannot be taught, but that it can be learned. Here I have to nod – but not all that sympathetically – to those hundreds of highly paid teachers of 'creative writing' courses in universities, mostly in the USA, but spreading now in all directions. In my experience, shown nakedly here, they are going about it the wrong way, peddling goods that are badly labelled and substandard in quality.

By far the best way to learn how to be a writer is to do it yourself – writing is hard graft. It requires hours of your day and days of your week and most years of your life, and it usually tires you out and has a harmful effect on your social life. And there is a necessary hinterland, also time-consuming and asocial: you find yourself reading a lot of books. All this constitutes more or less the first hurdle to be straddled and it is often here that most intending writers fall. Commitment is needed. Your interest must be genuine, not a passing fancy, or a misguided hope that having a book published will enhance your career, flatter your social standing or improve your sex life. Writing is a profession. You have to keep at it, even when you feel tired or disappointed or stuck. You have to be able to put up with your own company for hours on end. There is little or no money in it. All this is what I did. It is also what most other successful writers have done. There really is no alternative.

However, writing does not happen in isolation. The concept of the ivory tower or the penurious garret is a myth. Writers write in the real world, the ordinary world. They write between trips to the supermarket or the dentist, when they feel ill, when they feel randy, when they are broke, when they have driven somewhere all night, when they are happy, when they are cold, bored, flatulent, travelling, exhilarated, tired, disappointed, hungry, stuck ... and every other quotidian experience or happening.

So I felt that this instructive account required a context, and have therefore taken the fairly unusual step of describing a period of my life in some detail. It is quite long, which you might have already realized from flicking ahead through these pages to find out when the first story is going to appear.

It's not an autobiography: too much is left out for that to be true. In spite of what I say here about committing so many days in the week to writing, and so on, I was leading a fairly normal life of a young man with a job and a girlfriend, and most of that is not described.

I have concentrated on the elements of my life which do seem to me, when brought together, to be relevant to my becoming a writer. That is the point of the long preamble.

Everything in these opening pages is therefore directly or indirectly related to writing, and even the several digressions into other matters ultimately have a bearing on the main subject. Bear with them, even if the point seems temporarily to have been lost. Everyone's background is different, so there are no general rules here about how to become a published writer. If you happened to have missed the heady delights of growing up near Stockport, as I did, don't worry. We all have to come from somewhere. William Shakespeare was born in Warwickshire, as were John Wyndham and Rupert Brooke. Ernest Hemingway was born in Oak Park, Illinois. John Fowles came from Leigh-on-Sea, Graham Greene from Berkhamsted, Thomas Pynchon from Glen Cove, New York.

And, of course, the converse of my negative literary background is not true: nocturnal experiences at Eton or Harrow do not disqualify you, and alcoholics, Amazonian explorers, lapsed Catholics, etc., are always welcome.

In my case the only experience I can pass on is my own. I hope it's that general context which will be interesting in itself, but more to the point will provide some encouragement to people who might find themselves in a similar situation now.

ii

I sometimes felt I was not born to be a writer. My background is suburban, average, comfortable, stable, petty bourgeois, lacking in artistic traditions or even interests, what millions of people in Britain instinctively recognize as lower middle class. The time was in the summer of 1943, with World War 2 still fully engaged; the place was called Heald Green.

Originally a small village, during my childhood Heald Green was slowly being encroached on from the north by the expansion of Manchester, and from the east by the mill town of Stockport. These days, Stockport has been given the prefix 'Greater' and Heald Green has been absorbed into it. I come from a family of tradesmen and domestic servants – my father Walter began his career as a salesman and gradually ascended to managing director of the only company he worked for throughout his life, while my mother Millicent, orphaned at an early age, had been trained from childhood to work as a domestic paid companion. Both were from London – my father was born in a street that's now part of the perimeter road for Heathrow Airport, my mother in Barnsbury, in north London.

I have no literary antecedents and as far as I can tell there was not even much family tradition of reading. My parents were certainly not habitual book readers. My mother liked to read an occasional Agatha Christie thriller, but my father never read anything at home except the *Daily Express*. My two sisters and I were supplied with a dutiful ration of children's books, but it always felt to me as if I was the only one who was passionate about reading. I read and re-read and re-re-read the copies we had.

A love of reading was therefore my only deeply laid qualification for becoming a writer, and it's hardly unique. Another poor quality of my background is that I had gone through childhood and adolescence without showing much interest in life as a general proposition, not just in a literary sense but in every other sense. I disliked school and it got the worst out of me. I was idle and unmotivated and could not be stirred into academic activity. For most of the years at school I was near the bottom of the class with the 'rezzies' – Cheadle Hulme School was partly constituted as a charitable foundation for orphaned working-class children, and in those immediate post-war years Manchester had a lot of working-class orphans. Most classes had a dozen or so foundationers mixed in with the bright, exam-passing, middle-class day children. (I had been bright enough to pass the exam, but the light dimmed soon after.) These boarders or residents, rezzies, usually did badly in class. Few of the rezzies did as consistently badly as me, though – I was almost invariably in the bottom three.

Nor did I compensate for this with sporting prowess. I was hopeless at games, hated having to try and could never see the point of being in a team. I still can't. Throughout my last two or three years at school I kept remembering that old saw of parsons and uncles, that your schooldays are the best days of your life. If that was truly the case, I reflected, I didn't have much to look forward to. However, I wasn't a particularly morose child, just a bit of an awkward sod, and I always suspected the uncles and parsons were likely to be wrong.

Overall I simply had a bad time and couldn't wait to leave. In the last few months, when I had to take 'O' Levels, I did belatedly put on a bit of a spurt and tried quite hard, but it was too little too late. I took seven subjects. I was rewarded with five passes, but I knew that at least three of them would have been only marginal passes.

The two subjects I failed, some might be interested to know in view of later events, were General Science and English Literature – science and fiction, if you please.

The prospects for 'A' Levels and a university career did not look good, but fate was to take a hand. My father, who by this time was a director of his firm (which manufactured industrial weighing machines and scales), was promoted again and our family moved from Cheshire to the London area.

This turned out to be a crucial event. For most of the 1940s and 1950s my father had been running the Manchester office. As a child of Londoner parents growing up near Manchester, I had learned early about the alienating effect of having the wrong regional accent. When I was six I went to a primary school close to Wythenshawe, a huge postwar slum-clearance housing estate. I received a lesson in physical and mental bullying that removed every last vestige of inherited 'Londonness' from me within the first week. But ten years later, when we moved down to the south of England, I felt I had to go through the whole process all over again and shuck off my *ee bai gum* accent.

This relocation was in 1959. We were to move to a small house in the dormitory village of Doddinghurst, in the flat but pretty countryside just north of Brentwood, Essex. For myself and my younger sister it meant moving away from our friends and everything we knew. This meant little to me, because I was still an awkward sod who did not have many close friends, but I think it was more of a problem for my sociable sister.

At the end of the school summer term in 1959 I was therefore confronted with an unwelcome choice about what to do next. We were still in Cheshire, but we all knew that the move to Brentwood was just a matter of waiting for the new house to be completed.

Brentwood School was academically the equivalent of my old school, and I could have joined their Sixth Form for the two years of 'A' Levels. I didn't think much of that idea for several reasons. One was that Brentwood School was for boys only and after the mixed-sex Cheadle Hulme School I was used to the civilizing presence of girls. Another reason, as I discovered from an early visit to the town, was that the boys of Brentwood School had to wear straw hats. I didn't like the idea of wearing a boater at all. Most compelling, though, was the fact I was fed up with school.

The alternative, proposed by my father (whom I now realize was probably as irritated with my attitude as every other adult I knew), was to give up school altogether and find a job. He proposed what seemed for a few minutes to be a reasonable compromise between paid work and further education. He had discovered that my five mediocre 'O' Levels were enough to get me into accountancy as an articled clerk, and that the five years of professional training with a firm of chartered accountants were the equivalent of a university degree. I'd also be paid a salary.

It seemed like an answer and for someone with my passive approach it was easy to decide. My father found me two jobs, in fact. The first was a temporary job as an audit clerk with a firm of accountants in Manchester, in the six summer weeks before we moved to Essex. They paid me a weekly wage based on £150 a year: less than £3 a week. Even in 1959 that was a token amount.

At the end of my first week in the job in Manchester, a significant event occurred. As I left the office to go home I was handed a slim brown envelope containing my wages and I walked out of the building into the sunlight. I slipped the envelope open. Inside were two one-pound notes and a handful of coins. It was more money than I had ever had in my life. A heady sensation of untold wealth coursed through me. At that exact moment there was a terrible noise, a screeching of tyres and the sound of a vehicle collision, and suddenly everyone was shouting angrily at me. While I counted my money I had walked neglectfully into the rush-hour traffic of Deansgate – the car that braked to avoid me had missed me by a fraction of an inch and another car had slammed into its rear.

In later years, when my books started being published and I was again being paid trifling sums and the reviewers were, as it seemed, all yelling at me at once, I sometimes remembered that sunny afternoon in Deansgate.

iii

At the beginning of October 1959 I took up a more permanent appointment with an accountancy practice in London. I would be articled to one of the partners for a minimum period of five years. This meant that I could not change jobs in this time, but (more importantly, as things turned out) neither could they fire me. Under this Dickensian arrangement they would pay me a miserly amount, but they would train me for free. The firm was called Wright Stevens & Lloyd and my starting salary, which in practice was to be my continuing salary for a long time to come, was £250 a year. At first this paltry sum seemed unpaltry, after my time in Deansgate, but of course now I was living in the London area and faced with stiff commuting expenses.

WS&L's office was in Norfolk House, situated in a side street called Laurence Pountney Hill, which ran south from Cannon Street, at the Monument Underground station end. As soon as you were away from the traffic in Cannon Street, a comparative silence fell. The narrow lane led down between high office buildings, and a pub called the Cock and Bottle. Just beyond the pub the lane widened, and here was a chaos of cars and motorbikes, parked higgledy-piggledy in the tiny available space. There was a small garden behind the cars, always overgrown, but a haven of peace amid all the offices. Norfolk House was beside the garden.

If you went further down Laurence Pountney Hill into Suffolk Lane you came to Upper Thames Street, which ran close to the river.

The suite of offices on the third floor of Norfolk House was small.

There were separate rooms for each of the partners, and a larger office for the typists and the filing cabinets – four young women worked here, bashing strenuously at immense manual typewriters with carriages about a yard in length.

The largest room was the general office, dominated by a boardroom table with chairs all around the edge, and two or three large cupboards where the clients' bundles of tax papers or accounts records were kept. It was in this room that the routine work of checking or compiling figures was carried out by the articled clerks. At one end was a small desk and this was where a young woman worked alone, using a Comptometer manual calculating machine.

The other articled clerks were also male, teenagers or young men. They all apparently had a working grasp on accountancy, while I had only the vaguest idea of what was involved. Not much of my experience in the Manchester firm had rubbed off on me. On the day I arrived I was the youngest employee in the firm, just a few weeks past my sixteenth birthday.

My new colleagues were from London or the Home Counties. My parental background was also Londoner but I still had the undisguisable northern accent that the denizens of Shadow Moss Primary School had beaten into me. Most of the other young men had 'A' Levels, and one or two of the older ones had degrees – I of course had only my five scraped-through 'O' Levels. Almost without exception these well-spoken young men had been to single-sex public schools with conservative values, while I was from a co-educational grammar school which for all its many other failures, as I saw them, had at least ingrained in me an open-minded and liberal outlook, and a familiarity with the company of the opposite sex.

My obviously more affluent new colleagues were interested in the cars they drove, the team sports they played and the beer they drank in large quantities. Cars, sport and beer were subjects about which I knew nothing – my main interests were books and girls. To these other accountancy clerks a book was something that a book-keeper 'kept', and contained endless columns of figures. Girls seemed to be something variously called a 'sister' or a 'cousin' or a 'gel'.

Later I was to discover that at the weekends most of these well-heeled young men went off to something called 'the country', while I commuted daily from my parents' house in the Essex countryside. There was a shade of difference there that I did not immediately grasp. It didn't take long for me to understand; the English class system was in good order still.

I was therefore an outsider from the moment I arrived on the first morning, and remained so for the rest of my time in accountancy. It was a role I was used to after my awkward showing at school, and a few years later, when I became a writer, the habit of feeling myself to be outside the lives of others became an extremely handy one.

What I had not expected on my first day in the office was how fundamental my ignorance about accountancy actually was. Nor had I anticipated my inability to learn it. This was not just a craft inability, so to speak, but social as well.

While at school I had developed an abiding dislike for people who were having a 'good school', the ones who knew the words to the school song, who became monitors, who called teachers by their nicknames to their faces, and so on. I quickly found that the same types were working for this firm, having a 'good accountancy' in other words.

At the end of my first week, two of the 18-year-olds went out to celebrate the fact they had passed an intermediate exam. They did not go out for dinner, they did not get drunk, they did not seek fallen women, they did not even visit a cinema or theatre. They went to a hat shop and bought bowler hats. They returned with their expensive purchases and paraded solemnly around the general office, their new bowlers set at jaunty but impressive angles.

I felt a desperate need to escape.

Another kind of defining moment happened in the first minutes of my first morning. I was assigned to work with a young man called John, who was about three years older than me. John had two large ledgers in front of him.

'Do you know how to cast?' he said, in a cut-glass accent, after we had been introduced and were sitting side-by-side.

I looked and felt blank. To me casting was an activity involved with actors, or just possibly it was something anglers did. I knew nothing about either. 'No,' I said.

John threw down his pencil in mock despair.

'My God!' he said in a voice loud enough to be heard all over the general office. 'Don't they teach you people anything at those funny little schools in the north?'

Humiliated, I had to allow him to show me how to cast a column of figures. Within two seconds I realized that 'cast' was accountancy jargon for 'add up'.

As I have just discovered in the *Collins English Dictionary*, 'compute or calculate' is the forty-sixth meaning of the word 'cast'. There are forty-nine meanings in all, so it's pretty low down the long list of variant meanings.

I spent the rest of that day casting columns of figures in one of those ledgers. I actually spent the rest of that week casting columns of figures ... and, now I think about it, I spent much of the next seven years casting columns of figures.

Apart from casting figures, which needless to say was a boring and demeaning task, I soon learnt something else about accountancy. I genuinely didn't understand it or why anyone did it.

Worse, I didn't understand *money*.

I knew how to receive money, how to spend money, how to count money, and I had learned how to add up a column of it. I could open a savings account, write cheques, even borrow from time to time. But I never understood bills of exchange, borrowing patterns, business plans, corporate finance, debenture stocks, preferential shares, balance sheets. Even now, trying to remember what it was I didn't understand back then, I feel a fog of miserable incomprehension rising around me. I grew to hate money, in the sense accountants used it. It made me feel stupid and incompetent.

I was obviously no more destined for accountancy than I had been for an academic career.

So let us leave this barely 16-years-old version of myself, an unhappy adolescent, while he casts an endless column of figures. We can revert to more interesting subjects. Those are, of course, books and writing and literature.

iv

Although my parents were not bookish, I know that as a family we must have owned at least some copies, because I still possess a few of the children's books from that era. I and my sisters shared the books that came into the house, but during that period there was nothing like the proliferation of children's titles that are published in the present day. My early childhood was during the austere days of the late 1940s and early 1950s, when paper was rationed and books were few. In any case, I suspect my parents did not have much spare cash for books. Of course, we borrowed from the local library, but for the same post-war reasons there was not a lot of choice.

Reading was the one passion in my life, the only thing I actually enjoyed doing. Like all boys then I made model aircraft, I played with trains, I started collections of stamps, of cigarette cards, of match book covers, but my interest in this sort of thing was always fitful. I gravitated again and again to books, and would sometimes spend most of a weekend lying on my bed, reading one title after another.

I realize now that the mix of an obsessive interest in books and a dysfunctional life in the real world is a common background for writers. But when I was 14 all I knew was that I loved books.

Otherwise the world was out to get me. The non-book world made me learn Latin, it made me fall over in cold muddy playing-fields, or made me go shopping with my mother and sisters, or made me visit elderly relatives with alarming or terminal diseases. It was easy to prefer one way of life over the other.

Most of the books I read at this time were conventional children's fiction: I read fairly broadly and of course indiscriminately, and it's difficult from this distance to remember titles or all the authors' names. But I know I read the planetary novels of C. S. Lewis, the short stories of H. G. Wells, the Sherlock Holmes series by Arthur Conan Doyle and the flying and spy stories of Capt. W. E. Johns. I also scoured through the astronomy articles in Arthur Mee's *Children's Encyclopaedia*.

I remember in particular many of the books by Enid Blyton, who was in her heyday at the time. Blyton was a rather despised figure, then as she is now, so her books were always something of a guilty pleasure.

She is usually criticized (justly) for two literary shortcomings: a poor vocabulary, and English middle-class attitudes and prejudices.

Years later, as an adult writer, I came across the remarkable correspondence between Enid Blyton and an academic psychologist, Professor Peter McKellar. McKellar was interested in what he called a 'writer's imagery process'. Clearly having spotted something in Blyton's work he wrote to her for any information on the subject she could impart. She responded enthusiastically and at length, describing her use of eidetic imagining and her interest in hypnagogic imagery. The correspondence continued for nine fascinating letters. Reading these letters I realized that at last I had an explanation for the way in which many of Blyton's images from her stories lodged themselves so firmly in memory. I had always found her books memorably 'visual', and I also knew that these images were far more important and enduring than the poor use of language that the stick-in-the-mud librarians and critics complained about. It certainly explained her popularity with children.

For me it was the confirmation of something I had always instinctively known, about the fundamental importance of the use of the eidetic imagination by writers. If not by all writers, then certainly by me.

I try to make very few claims for my own writing, but the one I have always held to (at serious risk of mockery from stick-in-the-muds) is the knowledge, gained from my belated reading of the McKellar/Blyton letters, that she and I write in the same way. Everything she said about dreams, memories, imagination, sleep-wake thinking, visualization, was close to what I knew I had been doing from the moment I began writing. I had probably been doing it all my life, but only when I started writing did it become clear how much a part of my personal make-up this kind of visualized thinking was, and still is.

Memorable images or not, no child can read Blyton for longer than a couple of years, and by the time I was about ten or eleven I had started looking around for more meaty material. In the mid-1950s books were becoming more plentiful in the shops and paperbacks were on sale. As I entered my teens, I began spending my pocket money on paperbacks, and gravitated towards non-fiction books about the Second World War.

These books satisfied the curiosity that had been aroused by the many events I had heard my parents discussing with their friends, and which during the 1950s were constantly revived on television. The war was both familiar and tedious to me, but at the same time intriguing and mysterious. The scars of its impact on Manchester were still visible everywhere in the inner suburbs of the city.

I soon became intensely interested in WW2, and responded with a sense of thrill to the accounts of prisoners-of-war trying to escape through tunnels, bomber crews blowing up dams or dropping incendiaries on German cities, fighter pilots attacking the Luftwaffe, tank gunners sweltering in the Libyan desert, artillerymen escaping from Dunkirk, nurses sewing up the wounded, and so on. War books horrified and appalled me with their profane language, vivid descriptions of indiscriminate death and destruction, and memorable acts of bravery or self-sacrifice. In small stages I was being persuaded of the futility and wastefulness of war, a belief I have held ever since and which grows stronger year by year. Reading war books was just a teenage phase, but it was an intense one that cast a long shadow over my life and ideas.

War reading gave me an interest in books about aviation, and this led me indirectly to a non-fiction work by the American writer, Guy Murchie. I read his *Song of the Sky* during the summer weeks I was working in Deansgate, and it had a potent and lasting effect. The book is an extended essay about the sky, all aspects of the sky: clouds, winds, birds, gossamer spiders, gliders, thermal currents, thunderstorms. It is written factually but in beautiful and at times lyrical English. I was to re-read *Song of the Sky* several times more in the years that followed. It is the single most influential and inspiring book I have ever read. It has been out of print for many years, which is a shame. It is a masterpiece.

That was more or less where my reading was up to when I left the north of England to become a trainee accountant in London.

V

Something of a hiatus in reading followed the start of my doomed career in accountancy, because for the first few weeks and perhaps months I was swept up by the demands of having to try to learn the job.

I soon discovered that accountancy was not a static job, in which everyone worked permanently in a single central office. Accountants are surprisingly itinerant. Most of the work involves audit visits to other people's factories and businesses. Many of WS&L's clients were in different parts of London, but a number were based in the provinces and an audit of their books involved stays of several weeks or months in pubs or inexpensive hotels, often including weekends away from home.

These away trips were in general unpopular because they disrupted home and social life, but as a lowly junior trainee I was not in a position to negotiate. I soon found I was spending at least half of my time in distant towns, doing a job I disliked and didn't really understand.

For instance, within a few weeks of starting the job I was despatched to Ruthin, a small town in a windy part of North Wales, where I was to spend the next six weeks (not including a short break for Christmas) freezing to death in an unheated office next to a quarry. Other away trips followed at regular intervals, not all of them as physically uncomfortable as the first.

There were some advantages too, which can be summed up as being those enjoyed by a teenage male on the loose a long way from home, but there was never as much of that sort of thing as we always boasted about when we periodically returned to the London office. A weekend kicking your heels in the Kings Hotel in Grantham, Lincolnshire, was not quite as much fun as we tried to make out later.

As a committed and habitual reader I always had several books with me wherever I went but the time I could make free for reading was restricted. When I was working in the London office I read avidly during the daily commute by train from and back to Brentwood, but staying in small hotels with other articled clerks usually meant having to spend most evenings in their company. This was not what I wanted to do, but I learned more about cars, team sports and beer than I thought possible.

My taste in books was changing. I grew tired of war memoirs and went back to fiction, but now I was too old for children's books. I developed an interest in horror and read *Dracula* and *Frankenstein* (with mixed reactions – both novels are memorable, but they are also a bit of a slog to get through). I found anthologies of horror stories and worked my way through the classic short stories by the best writers in the genre.

I loved the stories of Ambrose Bierce, Algernon Blackwood and M. R. James – especially James, whose stories really frightened me. Then I discovered the novels of Dennis Wheatley and read them one after the other, with a complete lack of critical awareness. I read H. G. Wells's *The War of the Worlds* and Orwell's *Nineteen Eighty-Four*, in both cases approaching them with the belief they were horror novels. They can be seen that way if you're seventeen.

In July 1960 I was due to go on holiday to Cornwall with my parents. In those days it was possible to avoid much of the holiday traffic if you left your bed in the small hours and set out before the sun came up. I knew therefore I was in for a long journey in the back seat of my parents' car. On my way home from work I bought a book to read. It was John Wyndham's *The Kraken Wakes*, in its Penguin edition. I knew nothing of the book, or of Wyndham, but I liked the cover drawing of egg-shaped monsters snatching their victims with sticky tentacles. On the back it said that the book had been serialized by BBC radio. Once again I assumed it was a horror novel.

Before going to sleep I read the first chapter (the one where icebergs come floating up the English Channel) and a few hours later, as we drove through the dawn on Salisbury Plain and there was enough daylight to read by, I started on the rest. I was soon deeply involved with the novel, finding it a fast-moving, intelligent, subtle and exciting read. It clearly wasn't the usual kind of horror novel. It was a cut above Bram Stoker's turgid prose in *Dracula*, more up-to-date than Wells, less depressing and political than Orwell, more comprehensible than Mary Shelley's *Frankenstein* ... and as for Wheatley, although it was admittedly the same sort of thing as some of his novels, it was about a thousand times better.

I had no one around me to tell me that John Wyndham was one of Britain's leading science fiction writers. The Penguin blurb on the book was coy on the subject.

We stopped in Exeter for lunch. I went to a bookstore and bought every Wyndham book they had in stock. I read these during the remainder of the holiday in Cornwall. I enjoyed them so much that at the end I was frustrated to realize that I had used up more or less all the available supply of Wyndham's novels and short stories.

Back at my job, I returned to less compulsively interesting books, and soon I was travelling again to accountancy clients in distant provincial towns like Leamington Spa, Stevenage, Chester and Leighton Buzzard. During this period I was always reading fiction, but the only title I can remember for sure is Robert Sheckley's brilliant short-story collection *Pilgrimage to Earth*.

One winter's day at the beginning of 1962 I was sent to a rag-trade warehouse in the East End of London and settled down to what seemed in prospect several weeks of casting columns of figures. By this time I had become a relatively responsible caster-up of columns and had been put in charge of an articled clerk called George, who was newer and younger than me. On the first morning of the audit George and I worked unenthusiastically for a few minutes, then as boredom set in we began chatting.

Almost immediately I discovered that George had even less interest in cars, sport and beer than me. George was a fellow book reader! What was more, and fascinating to discover, was that he read science fiction. He was a real enthusiast, recommending titles and authors and recounting the plots of his favourite novels. At first I told him that I knew nothing about SF and had never read any, but George was quick to point out that Wells, Lewis, Orwell, Wyndham and Sheckley were amongst the best SF writers, and even the loathsome Wheatley (George's phrase) could just about qualify to be included in the genre.

Uniquely amongst all the people I worked with in accountancy, George was as much a frequenter of bookshops as I was. We spent our lunch hours happily browsing. For me it was a welcome change from those tedious hours in some City pub sipping at lemonade shandy, while around me the conversation was all about upper cylinder lubricant or rugby union or how to tell best bitter from IPA.

Within a couple of weeks George and I had gone our separate ways, rarely to work together again in the months ahead, but he had left his mark. I became an enthusiastic reader of SF and for a long time read almost nothing else.

I liked most of what I read, and I read a lot. I was soon averaging two or three SF novels a week, as well as a steady diet of short stories. I read not only British science fiction but American too. I enjoyed them both while being able to tell there was a difference. American writers seemed to be on an advanced and technologically complex plane: they wrote about matters I thought technical and stimulating, with a lot of use of what seemed like authentic scientific or engineering vocabulary. British writers wrote about more familiar or softer subjects, and were stronger on style, characterization, landscape, memory, images and feeling.

Like many committed readers of science fiction, I was annoyed by the way the genre was misunderstood and misrepresented in the wider world. I believed a lot of people were missing the opportunity to read a number of unusual and interesting writers, simply because of a prejudice based, apparently, on film posters, comics and old TV shows.

That prejudice has never really changed in the years since, even though the images and ideas of science fiction have become familiar to almost everyone, the common currency of Hollywood, advertising, TV shows, and much else. Somehow, the stigma acquired from the sensationalist old American magazines still persists.

The best science fiction was written well and imaginatively, contained novel and challenging ideas, and gave the reader a satisfying literary experience that seemed to be in about equal parts simple enjoyment and cerebral stimulation. On the other hand I had to admit that the worst examples of SF were pretty terrible and did match up to the widespread prejudices. But why judge a kind of writing only by its worst examples? There weren't even that many rotten books, as in general the editorial standards set down by publishers were high.

Thinking back to this period of my life I can estimate that I read science fiction for a total of about three and a half years. During that time I read most of the great or important works that had appeared until that point, as well as a lot of mediocre stuff. The period runs from the beginning of 1962, when George first got me interested in the books, until the autumn of 1965.

At that point there was a significant change: I began reading manuscripts professionally for a publisher, and almost overnight I found I had little time for leisure reading. Certainly, because I was reading science fiction submissions, I was unable any longer to read SF for pleasure and my literary interests widened. I remember discovering

Graham Greene, Nicholas Mosley, Iris Murdoch, Ayn Rand, George Orwell, B. Traven, Stan Barstow, Kingsley Amis, Muriel Spark, Ernest Hemingway and F. Scott Fitzgerald at this time, and went on from there. I never read SF for fun again.

The point of this is that my entire experience of reading science fiction is therefore crammed into the last couple of years of my teens and a year or so after that. My knowledge of SF is many years out of date. Although I have necessarily read some SF since – through knowing other writers, because publishers have asked for opinions on manuscripts, and because from time to time I write reviews for the press – in general my knowledge of science fiction ends in the mid-1960s. I have felt out of touch with the material for years, and am unreliable on the subject.

Again I am getting ahead of myself. We return to the winter of 1962, when I was a teenager held in suspension between two opposing worlds.

On the one hand I was deep in the grip of a profession whose work I did not understand, which bored me and which I disliked. I had little in common with the people I had to work with. On the other, I was living in a mental and imaginative world of literature, constantly interested in books, thinking about them and stimulated intellectually by them in every available moment.

Books were still just a hobby, though, and I had a living to earn. The £4.16s.2d that Wright Stevens & Lloyd paid me every week (tax and national insurance were deducted from that) was a miserable pittance, but it was certainly more than I could imagine ever earning from books. After all, I was only a reader. I had no ambition to become a writer.

vi

I made a discovery one evening at home in Doddinghurst that is such an obvious one I am almost ashamed to describe it now. I realized that books were written by writers.

Under the terms of my accountancy articles, I was supposed to work for my slave wages during the days, and study the textbooks in the evenings. I had reluctantly signed up to a correspondence course with a firm called H. Foulks Lynch Ltd., whose tutors were leading me slowly from one dull and baffling subject to the next. Every evening, after a meal with my parents, I would retreat to my bedroom, close the door, and get out Messrs. Foulks Lynch's study materials. I would arrange these convincingly on my table and beside me on the bed, take the cap off my fountain pen, open my writing pad to a page which had plausible-looking writing to at least halfway down the open page ... and then of course I would take out the paperback I was currently reading, and lose myself in its pages.

This subterfuge against the unexpected incursion of a parent only went on during the weeks I was working in London, and therefore living at home. If I was staying in a provincial hotel while on audit, nothing like it was of course necessary. For all the annoying aspects of their class attitudes, the other articled clerks I worked with at least showed a decent lack of commitment to their own studying. The main difference between us was that they seemed already to have grasped what was going on, so that skipping a few evenings' study had little impact on their ability to do the job. I, on the other hand, needed all the help I could get, although my motivation was zero. As a result, I wasted a lot of time with them in bars, but whenever I got away from them I could read for as long as I liked. Books were all that mattered.

However, at home I had to be furtive. It was a pleasant enough way of getting through the evenings, but my languid description of it now hardly conveys the upheaval of my polarized inner life at the time.

Accountancy induced in me feelings of immense boredom, worry, incomprehension and dread of the future. This revulsion was a constant, but so too was my enjoyment of reading, and all the mental ferment that went on as a consequence.

One evening I made my epiphanic discovery about the writing of books. I suddenly realized that a book did not come spontaneously or mechanically into existence, like the product of an unseen industrial process. A book was the result of a comprehensible human activity: a writer sat down for hours on end, with pen and paper, or with typewriter, considered every sentence, every word, even every comma, making choices and decisions all the way. The story was made up, invented, told.

I looked at the cover of the book I happened to be reading that evening. It was a paperback I had bought a few days earlier: the Digit Books edition of Brian Aldiss's *Non-Stop*, with its famous catchpenny cover painting and its sensational but misleading blurb. I saw it in a wholly different light: it had been *made*. A writer had *written* it.

At that moment the die was cast. I too would be a writer. Nothing else would be good enough. It was within grasp, do-able, achievable.

A few moments later I realized that writers were probably paid to write books, and that with a little effort it was possible to earn a living doing it. These were secondary to the main revelation, but they cemented my new ambition: I would become a writer, I would go on to become a writer who was paid, and in the end I would become a full-time professional writer.

It was March 1962, I was 18 years old and life had a point at last.

With hindsight it seems such a natural evolutionary step. Becoming a writer would not only be congruent with the main passion in my life, it also offered an escape-hatch from the dreaded future threatened by accountancy.

There were, however, a few practical problems, not least of which was that I had never written a word of fiction or non-fiction in my life. My handwriting was awful, my typewriting skills primitive, my experience of the world narrow. I was only just starting to emerge from the dim incomprehension of being a bored adolescent. There wasn't much to go on.

I reckoned it might turn out to be a long haul, but nothing would deter me from it.

vii

The immediate consequence of the decision was that I became much more selective in what I chose to read. I had always known that certain books were better than others. Some were just good enough, as many books are. But there were others that could be actively enjoyed, and there were more, the select minority, that could be not only enjoyed but appreciated too. I carried on reading science fiction, but I already knew there were differences between certain writers.

For example there was Isaac Asimov and there was J. G. Ballard.

I had read some of Asimov's science books while I was at school. I remember being impressed by one called *Inside the Atom*, which had made nuclear physics intelligible in a way the teachers had not. I thought highly of Asimov as a writer.

When I began reading science fiction I was fascinated to discover that Asimov was known for his SF too. I started buying his fiction. Rather to my surprise I found it to be the opposite of his non-fiction. It was hard going. His books were long and complicated, they were interested in things that did not interest me, his characters were completely unbelievable, and in general his books were written in a prose style I found difficult to follow. I kept having to go back and re-read the previous paragraph, because I thought I had missed something.

The publishers used extravagant language to describe Asimov's books ('classic' was the word that appeared most frequently), so I thought it must be my fault and kept persevering. I was always glad to finish an Asimov novel, and although I dutifully thought of him as a 'classic' writer, within a day or two I could remember hardly anything about the book I had just finished.

Then there was J. G. Ballard.

At this time Ballard was a young writer living in the suburbs of west London, hardly known even within the world of SF. I came across a handful of his stories in anthologies, and each one made a lasting impression on me. I hunted through bookstores and the local library, but I could find no trace of any books by him. Later, I located a specialist dealer and I was able to buy two or three imported American paperbacks. From the prelims I learned that most of his work was appearing in SF magazines, so I sent off for some of those too.

Ballard's plots were weird and ambiguous, his characters highly stylized, his prose mysterious, beautiful and obsessive. His ideas involved non-Asimovian matters like memory, identity, existence, time, entropy, art, surrealism. Once read, a Ballard story could never be forgotten.

In my new enlightenment as a would-be writer, I recognized what the difference between them really was, at least as far as I was concerned.

The kind of fiction Asimov was writing was a blind alley, a dead end. It was derivative in style, politically conservative, sociologically consensual. He wrote about technology, empires, commerce and power. He wrote about 'the future', but it was the sort of future I was desperately hoping to avoid. Asimov's fiction was a blank wall to other writers, especially young ones seeking inspiration.

Ballard, on the other hand, was radical, risky, open-source. He gave disturbing, unusual insights into the present day and the future he dreamed about was one in which the images of Dali, the ideas of McLuhan and the language of the space age would be employed. He unlocked doors that no one had even known were there before.

This did not mean that I wanted to write like Ballard, but that I could learn from him, make use of his example and find doors of my own to kick open. I gained nothing from Asimov, just an impression perhaps of the author's self-satisfaction. His books sent me to sleep in an imaginative sense. Ballard made me feel ambitious, creative, alert, connected.

J. G. Ballard was not the only writer who inspired me. Of the British writers I read at this time I liked Wyndham and Wells, John Christopher and the then-emerging Brian Aldiss. They were all recognizably within the SF genre, but also seemed to me to be better than the norm in different ways. Of the many Americans, I enjoyed the works of Robert Sheckley, Kurt Vonnegut Jnr, Frederik Pohl, Algis Budrys – again, they were all interestingly cross-current. I still read books from all strands of the SF genre, but these were the writers I found provoked ideas in me.

viii

A year went by. It was one in which I was constantly obsessed with the thought of becoming a writer, and putting the ambition into practice. My first attempts at writing fiction were revelations to me – I had no idea how hard it was to write even a simple sentence that would make sense as fiction.

I can never forget the very first story I tried to write, using a ballpoint on a pad of the columned analysis paper I had stolen from the accountancy firm's stationery cupboard. The story began (oh, hell) with an attempt to describe a spaceship in orbit about a planet, preparing to descend to the surface. I got as far as 'The –', but then I ground to a halt.

What came next? The *what?* How could I describe it?

'The spaceship' ...?

'The orbiting spaceship' ...?

'The ship' ...?

'The multi-generational starship which for eight thousand years had been crossing the wastes of space, while its occupants reverted to barbarism' ...?

I hadn't imagined that that sort of thing would be so difficult! Even the 'The' began to look unconvincing. I tentatively added a couple of words, then a few more. I struggled on for half a page, with more words crossed out than not, before I finally gave up. The story was never finished, and indeed it was barely started.

I began subscribing to a monthly magazine called *The Writer* and in my impatience sent off for all the back copies they had remaining in stock. They also published several books on the subject and I bought some of those. I found some *Teach Yourself* titles in my local branch of W. H. Smith, and bought those too. I scoured everything I could find, looking for advice, tips, serious guidance.

None of them ever mentioned science fiction, a fact that confounded and amazed me. At that stage, a science fiction writer was what I wanted to be. I didn't want to know how to research historical periods, I didn't want tips on bicycle rides to find locations, I didn't want the suggestion that I should sit on a double-decker bus with my notebook, ready to write down overheard conversations.

I wanted to know how to make people dream the way J. G. Ballard made me dream. I wanted to know how you evoked that other-worldly sense of weirdness in the most everyday of situations, just as Algis Budrys did. I wanted to know how to write witty, stylish sentences, like Brian Aldiss.

The writers' magazines, the writers' books, were hopeless on these subjects. Why had the people who wrote them never heard of science fiction? If it was mentioned it was done so in passing, sometimes mockingly or contemptuously, and invariably from a position of unassailable ignorance.

It was already plain to me that the SF genre was unique in its scope for serious writing, its responsive and intelligent readership, its creative possibilities for writers, even its lively commercial market. It was a substantial publishing genre, one actively seeking new work and developing young writers, one that paid reasonable rates and commanded a significant overseas rights market. By the beginning of the 1960s, just about every mass-market paperback imprint in Britain had a regular science fiction selection, publishing not only the American pre-war classics, but new writers too. Some of them were even British. At this time Brian Aldiss was regarded as the leading British SF writer, a point I concurred with, but why wasn't J. G. Ballard being published too? (*The Drowned World* had in fact been published in hardcover in 1962, with some wonderful story collections soon after – Ballard paperbacks did eventually appear from British publishers.) There were also regular magazines carrying SF stories – three magazines were being published in Britain at this time, J. G. Ballard's work cropping up constantly, as well as half a dozen or more titles in the USA.

All this work was serious or seriously intended, flourishing in an active commercial context. No other literary genre could compare with it. It was there on the bookstalls for everyone to notice and find, but presumably those lurid cover paintings were a deterrent. All people had to do was see behind them, open the pages, remember the old saying about not judging a book by its cover. I already knew that science fiction readers were a minority, albeit a consistent, motivated and highly active minority. But these people who wrote how-to books on writing were as ignorant of science fiction as everyone else. I soon realized I could learn nothing from them. Anyway, why had I never heard of a single one of these self-professing literary experts? They claimed to know everything but their names were obscure and their intelligence about writing matters restricted to the same old unadventurous clichés.

Meanwhile, constantly aware of the steep climb to excellence that lay ahead of me, I struggled on with my own awful attempts, finishing none of them.

One failed story I remember was about a planet where time ran backwards: the only person who didn't realize what was happening was my central character. I got him down to the surface of the planet (somehow!), and then tried to make him say something.

Dialogue! It was impossible to imagine what someone, *anyone*, would say if he landed on a planet where time was running backwards. Would he speak backwards? Would everyone else? Anyway, what would they talk about?

'Did you have a good flight in your spaceship?'

Or maybe: 'Spaceship your in flight good a have you did?'

Or maybe even: '?Pihsecaps ruoy ni thgilf doog a evah uoy did'

It was unassailable, hopeless. Worse was the thought of what might be said in reply. And would anyone understand it? Would anyone want to read it?

Not long into this discouraging experience I learned something useful at last from one of the writers' guides.

Editors, the book said, expected all manuscripts to be typewritten. It was no good sending in anything that was handwritten. (Or on accountancy analysis paper, I dare say.) I was astonished, because I had been working hard on my untidy handwriting, trying to make it more legible before I was ready to submit any stories. Didn't Walter Scott and Charles Dickens and H. G. Wells write in longhand? Well, perhaps that was too long ago.

Anyway, I felt a surge of optimism at this news, because my parents owned an old Olivetti Portable they never used, and when I was at school I had worked on it briefly to learn typing. Like everything else I did at school I had entered into it half-heartedly, so I had never taken things as far as learning how to touch-type, but at least I was familiar with the machine. I found it, cleaned and oiled it, bought a new ribbon for it.

I had done something right at last.

I sat on the edge of my bed with my new typewriter on my knees and began typing out with two fingers the last terrible draft I had been essaying. It looked much better when it was typewritten. A few sentences read as if I had known what I meant. Now even the bits I crossed out *xxxxxxxx*, looked like something a professional writer had changed his mind about. I regarded the results in a thoughtful way.

I mention all this to underline what a complete greenhorn I was.

I came into the world of writing from the bottom, the very bottom.

No writer has ever had fewer advantages than me. I am trying not to exaggerate in any way, to make things sound worse (or better) than they really were. The fact is that nothing came easily to me. I had to learn everything and I was painfully aware of the awfulness of what I was writing.

I knew no other writers. I had no one to give me genuine advice, to encourage me or discourage me. When I shyly mentioned my ambition to my girlfriend, she actually mocked me for it. I never talked about writing again to her, and not long afterwards changed girlfriends. My inner resolve had been stiffened by her mockery, of course, but the fact remained that apart from the despised how-to books I had no one to tell me what to do.

The more I thought about writing and everything surrounding it, the harder it seemed. But I never gave up. I worked at it endlessly, whenever I had a spare moment, whenever I felt it was worth another try.

In 1963 I was given two months off work for what was called 'study leave' – the first of several accountancy exams was approaching. When you see in a movie a scene where an inexorable horror is advancing on the characters, you might get a glimpse of the terror the prospect of accountancy exams induced in me. However, the study leave gave me time off work. I welcomed the break from the boring job and the stresses of commuting to London. I spent the time well at home: I had lots of SF novels to catch up with, lots of typing to do.

In due course I took the examination and inevitably failed. I don't think I was in the bottom three, but I could not have been far off. No bowler hat for me.

Winter approached again.

I was licking my wounds over the exam results, and smarting from the pep-talk I had had to endure from Derek Hinkley, my boss at the firm. I felt the claws of accountancy tightening endlessly around me, a pincer movement of immense tedium on one side and incurable poverty on the other. Mr Hinkley had informed me I wouldn't be given a raise until I passed the first exam, and the prospect of that was hopeless. I looked Mr Hinkley in the eye and conscientiously promised him that I would sort my life out and knuckle down to proper work.

And so I did. I suddenly thought of a story I felt I could write, one with a plot where I reckoned I could get to the end, one with a setting I believed I could manage to describe. I opened up the Olivetti and began to type.

A few days later I was roughly halfway through the first draft when there was a report that President Kennedy had been assassinated. That's where I was when I heard the news that reverberated around the world that day: sitting on the side of my bed in my parents' house, an old portable typewriter on my lap, a draft of my first finishable short story rolled around the rubber platen. I did no more writing that day in the face of the shocking news, but I returned to the story a few days later and I did manage to complete it soon after.

That story was called 'Going Native', and it is the first one in this book.

ix

It is time to come clean about the stories.

Most of the ones included here have never been professionally published before, but two or three were printed in magazines and have not been subsequently reprinted. They appear in chronological order, starting with 'Going Native' from November 1963, and finishing with a story called 'The Interrogator', which I completed in January 1968. So these stories cover a period of just over four years, during which time I slowly progressed from the state of being a complete novice to that of a professional writer. (I left my last job and became a full-time writer in August 1968.) These are the stories that mark that progress.

I have already described how 'Going Native' provided the necessary transition from the world of uncles, accountants and commuters. At the other end of the four years 'The Interrogator' did much the same, a few steps higher up.

I have more to say about what happened to this story, in the notes that follow it.

x

The stories in this book are best read as object lessons, I think. The context is all, which is why I have written so much here about my personal background. While they are not 'good' stories, undiscovered or recently unearthed gems that were previously thought lost, none of them is embarrassingly awful. Well, two or three of them do contain embarrassments, but I trust to the context to moderate that a little. And there's the fact that what embarrasses one person is often just amusement for someone else, and anyway maybe you won't spot them at all.

Each of these stories was seriously intended. That is, in different ways and at different times I thought of them as worth writing, worth showing to other people, worth hoping they might be published. The fact that in most cases I turned out to be wrong does nothing to change the original intent.

Much of what constitutes professional writing is good judgment – knowing what you can write within your ability, or how far you can try to stretch your ability, and then making a fair assessment of what publishers and editors are looking for at the time. Judgment comes with experience and so it hardly bears on new writers. All you can do is your best, when you can do it.

What stories are here in this book will be obvious by looking at the table of contents and by flicking through the pages that follow. The ones that are missing cannot be discerned, so let me describe the ones I decided to leave out.

The very first pieces of fiction I wrote pre-dated 'Going Native' by a few weeks. They were skits, little more than set-ups for puns, which were revealed in the final sentence. The intention, as with all puns, was to induce groans. I mention these half-page squibs for sake of completeness and I defend them for two reasons: firstly, there weren't many of them – maybe only two or three in all. Secondly, they were a way for me to practise. They were rather badly done, the jokes were terrible and unfunny, and from looking at my faded carbon copies I think even the typing was pretty dreadful. There's no point reviving them now.

'The Run' is not here, even though it came relatively early in this chronology – in August 1965, between 'The Witch-Burners' and 'Impasse'. 'The Run' was the first short story I sold, and therefore memorable in every way. The sale was to Kyril Bonfiglioli, who was editing a magazine first called *Science Fantasy*, then later called *Impulse*, and later still *SF Impulse*.

I have sometimes told the story of how Bon – who was to become a good friend, but in 1965 I had never met him – had held the manuscript of 'The Run' in its envelope for many months in what was even then a legendary mountain of unopened manuscript-sized envelopes. Aspiring writers sent their manuscripts to Bon after all other avenues had been explored. This was not because his magazine was no good – on the contrary, it was an attractive and witty publication, with many hits; Keith Roberts' brilliant novel *Pavane* was first published there, for instance – but because Bon appeared never to return any manuscripts. He either published the stories, or he left them unopened in his pile.

One evening, full of shyness, I phoned him up to ask if he had had a chance to read it. He responded immediately with the thrilling words: 'It's in the next issue!' He went away to confirm this, leaving me hanging on. In the distance I could hear what sounded like envelopes being hurriedly torn open. After Bon had returned twice to the phone – first to ask me to spell my name, then later to 'confirm' the title of the story – he came in triumph to say he had found my most excellent story and it was indeed scheduled for the next issue.

To this day I still wonder if he ever read it, but he eventually paid me £8.8s.0d.

'The Run' was anthologized once, by Judith Merril, in a book of British-based SF with the testicle-retracting title *England Swings SF*. Even back then in 1967 it seemed like a ghastly title for a book, but this was the era of miniskirts and flower power, and there was no discouraging an American editor in London, and her publisher in New York, who were determined to look trendy.

When the anthology was published in a British paperback, it was sensibly renamed *The Space-Time Journal*.

I later included 'The Run' in my own first collection of short stories, *Real-Time World*, and it thereafter achieved publication in several different languages. Its last known authorized outing was in 1986, when it was read on German radio, but since then an Australian website has been illicitly distributing a spoken-word recording. I can't help feeling that if the fiction bootleggers have reached down as far as 'The Run', then this illegal practice must be more widespread than I had previously imagined.

In 1967, Janet Freer, my newly appointed literary agent, suggested that a quick way of making money was to write some short-short stories for a popular British weekly magazine called *Tit-Bits*. In spite of the come-on title, parts of women's breasts were never actually shown, but otherwise the magazine plunged deep into trivial nonsense, a sort of early precursor of the celeb magazines of the present day. The editor of *Tit-Bits* was looking for SF at the time, so I wrote a short-short in an afternoon. It was bought almost as quickly as it had taken me to write. I then wrote another, which did not sell to *Tit-Bits* but which was eventually published in *Signature*, a magazine published by the Diners Club.

Neither of these two exercises in quickie fiction is in this book. They can no doubt be tracked down by diligent researchers at the British Library, or by burglars ransacking my mouldy old files in my office, but I don't want them reprinted here.

Before this, in early 1966, I wrote one of the few short stories I have ever undertaken as a collaboration with another writer. This was with Colin Pilkington, who was a frequent contributor to *New Worlds* under the pseudonym 'George Collyn'. At the time, Collyn was widely believed to be a pseudonym used by Michael Moorcock, but it was not. I met Colin Pilkington several times, and we agreed to write a story together.

I don't know why most collaborations take place, but I think I understand what happened in our case. I thought of Colin as someone who might provide me with an easy route to breaking into print. Meanwhile, I think Colin was seeing me as someone who would handily do all the drudgery of a first draft for him.

Anyway, a first draft is what I did, with much difficulty. I assumed Colin would then do a second draft and return it to me so that I could have another shot at it.

When he got down to it, Colin wrote an extended second draft which was so unlike my first draft that it might as well have been a different story. Before I could read it he submitted the top copy to Michael Moorcock at *New Worlds*, and sent me a carbon copy. Moorcock rejected it, but I still have the carbon copy. About 98% of it is Colin's work and the only traces of my efforts remain in details like characters' names. Four decades later I have no idea if it was any good or not, but I suspect from Moorcock's swift rejection that it was probably not. Colin died in 2002. The story was called 'They Closed the Door', and it's not in this book.

Also not here is 'No Ship of Easy Virtue', which by a long shot is the worst thing I ever wrote. I cringe to remember it. Although I have had to overcome a lot of cringing when including some of the stories which are in this book, none of that compares with the horrors for me of this story. It was 1,300 words long, I wrote it in a day in April 1967 and it was a day mis-spent. I should have burnt the thing as soon as it was finished. I did not, but now I have mentioned it here I think I might have to, in case the burglars come across it.

I have written other duds since, and there are at least three or four of my stories which have appeared in obscure publications, or only in translation and have not been anthologized in English. They all fall outside the period 1963-1968, so do not count anyway.

Those I've mentioned are therefore the only omissions from this book. Everything else I wrote in the period is here.

xi

The stories appear in the order in which I wrote them, irrespective of their dates of eventual publication (in the few cases where that applies). None of them has been rewritten. That is to say that I have not gone through and 'improved' them or brought them 'up to date'. Where I saw obvious spelling mistakes I corrected them. I left the original punctuation alone but in a few cases where the punctuation actually changed the meaning of what I intended, I have silently corrected it. Nothing has been omitted deliberately. Nothing has been added. All I have done is to go through and check for consistency of appearance, lay-out, punctuation and spelling conventions.

At the end of each story I have added a brief narrative, in two parts.

The first part is more or less what I knew about the story at the time I wrote it: what was in my mind when I wrote it, what I intended for it, where the idea might have arisen, what happened to it when I completed it, and that sort of thing.

The second is my present-day reaction to the story. This is not intended as a sly way of nudging the reader towards signs of alleged burgeoning ability ('look at this bit, which is surprisingly good – the kid obviously had promise'), nor is it an attempt to distance myself now from the follies of youth. I've tried to imagine what I would say if I saw the story as part of a writers' workshop manuscript discussion.

Perhaps a word of explanation about writers' workshops is needed. A workshop can be simply set up and run by a number of like-minded writers getting together for regular informal meetings, but increasingly workshops are administered by arts associations, colleges, libraries, and so on. Most of them have slightly different procedures but the essence of them all is criticism of manuscripts submitted by each participant, stated in a candid, uninhibited and constructive way. As everyone has a say, and everyone takes it in turn to be the recipient, a sense of charmed freedom of speech soon emerges, and a great rapport is likely to develop between all present. Workshops do not 'work' for everyone but most people seem to get a lot out of being in one, and often the heady state of creative gestalt is enough to give a big push of encouragement, whose momentum carries on in the weeks that follow. If a workshop is conducted properly it can be a useful discovery for beginning writers and an equally stimulating refresher boost for more established people. At a workshop, writers learn without being taught.

I never had the benefit of joining a writers' workshop when I was starting out, although I have been involved in several of them since. I have no idea what the real benefit to my writing would have been in the mid-1960s, but I am certain that had I known of the existence of workshops I would have run, not walked, to join one of them.

So, returning to these stories of mine, when I looked back at them I tried to think myself into that state of mind which produces a candid appraisal of the text that is there to be read, ignoring what I remembered of my hopes and intentions. In other words, I tried to look at them with a fresh eye.

More than four decades have elapsed since I wrote them, which I think is long enough for a measure of objectivity. Certainly, when I burglarized my ancient files and found the old carbon-copies, I encountered many surprises.

However, because detailed criticism of text can become tiresome after a while (except to the recipient, who normally soaks it up with feelings mixed between gratitude and irritation) there isn't too much of it in this book. There is just enough to convey the general idea, I believe. Maybe others will delight in adding their own, but I don't want to be sent them, thanks all the same.

If this book has a point it is to show that young writers have to start somewhere, that they can learn and improve, that the road is long but not *that* long. I also hope and intend that my efforts show it's worth giving your writing a serious attempt if it's what you really want to do. I stuck at it, and others can too.

I apologize for none of the stories here. I claim nothing for them either. These are simply the stories I wrote while I was learning how to be a writer.

Going Native

(NOVEMBER 1963)

It had all started about one Martian year before.

As I parked the sand-hopper in the shadow of the strangely asymmetrical artifact, I recalled the puzzlement it had given our pioneer explorers on Mars. On a world of cold featureless deserts, with occasional wild outcrops of rock, giving way to flat lichenous plains and the small ice-caps, the smooth whorls and cantilevered spans of the iron-grey construction had seemed unutterably misplaced. Of course, it was there for a reason and it hadn't taken the first Earthmen long to discover just what.

I jumped down from the hopper and walked stiffly to the now often-used portal. As usual, there was a sergeant on duty, and with hands skilled with long practice he operated the controls of the airlock. Surely, in the whole of the universe there could be no more beautiful, and yet somehow ungainly, airlock.

Once safely inside, I thankfully disencumbered myself of the spacesuit which I had worn for the past week. Even on low-gravity Mars, a 'suit can become a great burden after an extended period inside.

'Good to see you back, sir,' the sergeant politely observed, as he helped me out of the harness.

'Thank you, sergeant, I'm glad to be back in one piece,' I replied, remembering a rather worrying experience with an air cylinder. I had been out on a week-long geological survey of a relatively near rock outcrop, which had proved to be quite well sown with isotope traces. Our physicists should be pleased with this result, the Expedition had to be paid for.

The sergeant took my 'suit, and after signing the obligatory chit I made my way down to the Belt.

The Belt on Earth would have been a scientific sensation, on Mars it was a very much below-average commonplace. Once on it, I was swept speedily and noiselessly downwards, I knew this was so from the reports of our scientists, but otherwise I would not have known as there was no sensation of dropping whatsoever. To my eyes it appeared that the continuous Belt was pulling me inexorably onwards through a well lit and spacious horizontal tunnel. In fact, the Belt drops an exact distance of two thousand five hundred and forty-two point three metres over an exactly equal distance in a forward direction.

As my ride on the Belt neared its end, the tunnel roof rose higher and higher until looming up at me, at an apparent angle, I could see the whole of the City spreading before me. It was officially called, quite unimaginatively, Mars City, but the natives call it Parynko, as near as our language can manage it, and that is good enough for most of us.

Parynko is wonderful. No other word will fit the description of the one remaining inhabited city on Mars, acclaimed by some as the scientific mecca of the Solar System, its praises have been sung by every Earth scientist who has ever visited it. Biologist, physicist, anthropologist, chemist, none has ever found an apt superlative to describe it. *This* is the wonder of Parynko, almost every month a new marvel of science is turned up by our specialists, who use the technology so gained for the advance of our own civilisation. Why, the very vessel I came to Mars on, and the fuel it was powered by, was of Martian design, discovered in those tentative early days of the first explorers. But, however, even before this, those first nervous Americans had discovered a far greater enigma: the population of Parynko.

Numbering in all approximately two hundred thousand, the people of the City go about their business, as far as we can make out, in an uninterrupted fashion. They just don't care about our intrusion. Never over-friendly, never hostile, always polite and cheerful, the Martians seem to accept our presence as naturally as they do their own.

Fairly soon after the first Americans' arrival a large library was discovered, and with the aid of one who could only be called a librarian, and his assistants, the language of these odd people was soon learnt by our philologists. Gradually, more understanding was reached as the history of the planet began to unfold.

The library wasn't situated far from where the Belt deposits its riders, and consequently it was one of the first buildings I passed on my way to our now-permanent headquarters. Standing in the library entrance, fluently speaking the gentle melodic tongue of the Martians, Kenny Hawkins, one of our leading philologists, was talking with a small group of native children. I waved, and with smiles and calls the group replied. It's people like Kenny, I mused, who are making this venture the success it is.

Yes, our Martian expedition *is* a success. At no other time had I felt so firmly convinced. As I walked the kilometre or so to the headquarters I savoured the sights and sounds around me, which, after a week's absence, presented me with something reminiscent of my first-ever visit.

The traffic of ground-cars, hovering noiselessly a few centimetres above the ground, yet mysteriously chattering gently when they moved; the all-pervading resonance of the buildings, vibrant with a non-animate life of their own; the pleasant shades and hues of the clothes of the people; the spindly towers, soaring bridges and apparently frail spans of the architecture; but, above all else, the people. At all hours of the day the streets are alive with people, always smiling, calling to each other, walking, riding the ground-cars, wheeling their gaily coloured carriages, and generally living their lives to the full. Never once in all our stay in Parynko have we ever seen a hostile action, nor heard a voice raised in anger.

The one thing in particular that we have never grown accustomed to is the deference with which we are treated. Singly, if spoken to, the Martians are friendly and helpful, but as a race Martians just aren't interested in humans. Their one concern seems to be one of living out the heritage ordained for them by their ancestors.

On reaching our headquarters, I found my chief wasn't in, so I stowed my remaining gear and my case of samples behind his desk and went in search of company.

I found it in the shape of a party, already well under way in the bar, inevitably one of the first places to have been opened. As I went in the shout went up, 'Hallo, Dave's back,' and soon I was relaxing amongst friends and enjoying the party to the full.

Two hours later, I was discussing with a group of friends the problems entailed in forming an Officers' Club, when Bruce Clement quietly joined our circle.

'What's up, Bruce?' someone asked at the sight of his rather glum face.

'Nothing's really wrong, thanks,' he replied, 'I'm just a bit worried about Disodo. You see, he's gone.'

'What do you mean, gone? Walked out on you, has he?'

'Well no, not that, at least not as far as I can tell. His things are still in his room.'

'Perhaps one of his relations is ill,' somebody else suggested.

'I thought of that,' Clement replied, 'I've just been speaking to his brothers, but the funny thing was, they didn't seem to know who I was talking about. Whenever I mentioned Disodo's name they asked me to repeat it, as if they'd not heard it before. I suppose, incidentally, none of you have seen him?'

We all shook our heads. I of course hadn't seen Disodo since before I'd left. Bruce Clement was another of our philologists, and soon after he arrived he had struck up acquaintance with a young Martian boy, Disodo. For a time, Clement had lived with Disodo and his family, learning their ways and increasing the scope of his mastery of their language. After a while, Clement returned to our quarters and Disodo came with him, working for him as his personal servant. This arrangement did not last long, however, for Disodo was eventually more like a son to Clement than an employee.

And now, Disodo was gone.

We offered further suggestions to Clement, but none seemed to satisfy him and eventually he wandered off, presumably in search of Disodo.

Soon after that the party broke up.

As time went by, Disodo's disappearance was forgotten in the main by Earth-Base personnel. Clement, however, was deeply disturbed by the affair, and it changed his character quite markedly. The Bruce Clement of old had been cheerful and witty, with a pleasant turn of character, but now he became more withdrawn and seemed constantly puzzled. He spent long hours of his leisure time away from the rest of us, and it was rare indeed to meet him socially. His work, too, took a turn. He devoted his work to the study of the history of the Martian language and of the society generally. Indeed, it is through Bruce Clement's work in this field that we have learned much of what is now common knowledge. The reasons, for example, why the Martians live beneath the surface of their planet, what became of their surface-living ancestors, and how the atmosphere of Mars became the feeble, lifeless thing it is today.

I suppose that somewhere along this line, Clement evolved his theory about the Martians.

The time inevitably came when he propounded his ideas to his fellow officers. Of course, he was ignored.

His next step was to corner us, one by one, and work carefully on us until he had us half-believing him. Afterwards, thinking about it would result in our laughing it off, reason just wouldn't allow such a premise. So too, in the end, this way failed as well. Poor Clement just could not get anyone to go along with such an outrageous idea.

Bruce Clement had the courage of his convictions, and so determined was he that he was right that he couldn't let it lie. At every opportunity the subject was brought up. Singly, and as a group, we got heartily fed up with what was known amongst ourselves as 'The Clement Effect'. So, in order that group sanity be maintained, we laid a plot, craftily we arranged every detail until we were satisfied that all was perfect. The next time the subject was raised our plan was carried out, violently and enthusiastically.

Afterwards, saddened, a little sore, and certainly much wiser, Bruce Clement kept his peace.

Normal working and social conditions soon returned, and so, we hoped, had Clement's reason.

The rest of the Martyear passed relatively uneventfully, and Clement resumed his work on Martian history, such as that existed. He seemed to forget the affair about Disodo, and with it his high-flying notions about vaporizing Martians. Until yesterday.

Phil Masters and I were on our way down to the headquarters where a film-show had been laid on, and had dropped in at the recently-initiated Officers' Club for a quick drink beforehand. We were just finishing when Bruce came in, and by buying us a second round of drinks, neatly cornered us. Not that we wanted to avoid him, but Clement did have a reputation that he was still finding hard to live down. Even so, it had been some time since we'd last met him socially, and we had no desire to be rude.

He sat down quickly on an adjacent chair, and put his cap on the table between us. We exchanged pleasantries until finally, out of the blue, he said, 'Dave, pardon my opening an old wound once more, but I really must speak to someone about this. You remember Disodo? Well, one or two rather interesting –'

He stopped because I'd raised my hand. I *knew* all about Disodo, and didn't want to hear any more. 'Look Bruce,' I said, 'I think we've been through all this before. You're just making a mountain out of a molehill about that boy. He went away, changed his job. Granted, it's strange he never said anything to you, but there you are, there must be a perfectly reasonable explanation for it all. I think all these supernormal theories of yours are pointless.'

'Yes, but –'

'Excuse me interrupting, Bruce,' Phil put in quickly, 'but I'm not sure what's going on. I think I must have missed out somewhere.' At the time, Phil had in fact been with Arnold's group pushing its exploratory way through Syrtis Minor, and thus had been spared the brunt of Clement's notions. But now it seemed, Phil was in for the full treatment.

Much to my surprise, Clement was very concise, coming to his point almost immediately. He gave only a very brief outline of what had happened, and his theoretical interpretation of the facts. 'And then,' he finished, 'soon after Disodo had gone, and even while I was still making enquiries, one of his brothers vanished too. Just like that.' He clicked his fingers in the air. 'One day he was at home with the rest of the family, the next – gone. The funny thing was, that whenever I raised the point to his family, they looked blankly as if they'd never heard of the boys.'

'This much I know,' I said, 'and it can be quite easily explained away –'

'Yes, yes, I know all about that, the point is that I was never allowed to explain further ...' He looked at us, a rather appealing expression on his face, willing us to listen.

I sighed, 'All right, Bruce, I'll hear you out, never let it be said I didn't give you a hearing!'

Phil agreed. 'Mmm, me too, this sounds interesting.' Apparently, hearing the story from a fresh viewpoint had given Phil that extra edge of interest.

Clement's face took on an intense aspect, and he leaned forward in his seat. 'The thing that is most odd about all this is that his family, who must have held him in considerable affection, just did not seem to recognize his name when I mentioned it. Although they never denied outright his existence, neither did they acknowledge it. So, bearing this in mind I decided to keep an eye half-cocked in their direction, and occasionally I would drop round to their apartment. One day I went there and the whole family had gone! There was another family living in their apartment. *They've* never even heard of Disodo's family. Now, explain that!'

'I suppose,' Phil tried, 'they *could* have, quite simply, moved away, and –'

'No Phil,' Clement interrupted, 'that won't do, remember I was on friendly terms with them, and I'm sure it would have been mentioned at some time. No it's not quite a easy as that. Look, let me ask you something.'

'Fire away,' Phil said, 'I'll answer if I can.'

Clement took a deep breath, 'When you walk through the streets, what do you see?'

Phil thought for a moment. 'Well, there's the library, our headquarters, er ... those odd towers, the ground-cars, that great globe thing in the centre, er ... more?'

'Go on, you've hardly started.'

'Well what is it you want, I could go on all day?' Clement didn't answer. 'Oh, all right, there's the Belt, the Hall, the library, the ...'

Clement stopped him. 'You've had the library once. You might as well give up, you'll never get what I'm after, all you've done is to give me, and not very well either, a list of the buildings comprising the City. Buildings by themselves don't make a city, it takes something else.'

I felt it was about time I had something to say in this matter. 'I think I know what you're after, Bruce,' I said, 'you mean the people.'

'That's it. Good, now we're getting somewhere,' confirmed Bruce. He turned back to Phil. 'Now, what do you notice most about *them*?'

'Nothing really, they all look the same to me.'

'Phil, you've just hit the nail right and hard on the head. That's exactly what I wanted you to say. The crux of the matter is that, to us, all Martians look the same. It's the same back on Earth, I'll bet you can't tell a Japanese from a Chinese, or a Pakistani from an Indian. To an Oriental's eyes we westerners all look the same too: they swear blind that Occidentals are identical. It's an acknowledged fact that members of one race all seem alike to members of another.'

Now Phil was leaning forward too. 'Okay, I'll grant you that, but I don't see how it fits in with your theory.'

'No,' Clement corrected, 'I'm not trying to say it's a proof, it's merely an accessory to the idea. Now this is where things get really interesting, working on this I decided to try an experiment one day. I was walking down what we call Fountain Boulevard, I believe the natives call it Trylo, thinking along these lines when one particular Martian caught my eye. As we agreed just now, once you've got over the initial surprise of seeing alien life, you don't really notice Martians. They just seem to mix in with the general background. This particular one attracted my attention because he was wearing a scarlet shirt-like garment, and as you know, it's really very rare to see a Martian wearing a bold colour, they seem to prefer the softer shades.

'I wasn't watching this chap, mind you, it's just that every time I looked up he was still in sight, and noticeably so, too.

'When I reached the end of Fountain my path crossed the Park, and so it seemed, did Redshirt's. By now he was only about a hundred yards in front of me. All of a sudden, he swung sharply to the left and appeared to dodge behind one of those squat bushes that are dotted about the Park. It took me about thirty seconds to draw level with the bush, and mainly through curiosity I looked to see the Martian, There was absolutely no sign of him.'

'I suppose by "no sign" you mean you had a fairly comprehensive look-round for him?' Phil asked.

'Yes, with the exception of that bush, the Park is pretty bare round there and there was nowhere to hide. Also, as I said, my friend was unusually prominent, and in the Park there's no crowd to mingle with.'

Despite myself, I was impressed. Clement hadn't mentioned this the last time he'd propounded his theory, mainly because we'd never let him carry on so long. He hadn't finished yet, either.

'As I'm sure you can imagine,' he continued, 'I stayed in the Park for quite a time, making sure beyond all doubt that Redshirt had, in fact, vanished. Of this I am certain.

'Coming back from the Park afterwards, my mind was whirling at a fantastic rate. On an impulse I selected another Martian, this time a female, and kept my eye on her. Of course, she wasn't nearly as conspicuous as the first, but by keeping constant watch on her, I made sure of keeping track of her.

'Almost the first thing to strike me was the fact that she wasn't going anywhere. She walked, with me following discreetly, through the same sequence of streets four times. I was just telling myself that this was her sole occupation when, quite quietly, she wandered behind a stationary ground-car ... and disappeared!'

He waved a grubby notebook in our direction. 'Look,' he said, 'it's in here, I wrote down exactly how it happened the same night. There are dozens of other instances, too. You try it yourself, go outside, select a Martian, keep your eye on him, and I guarantee that within the half-hour he'll have gone!'

This was becoming outlandish. 'Now just hold it a minute, Bruce,' I said, 'we're getting rather ridiculous. At first I was half-convinced, but now –'

'I'm sorry, Dave,' Clement maintained, 'it does sound crackpot I know, but if you were to only try, I'm sure you'd be satisfied. You have to be careful though, if they know you're watching, they don't go.'

'Bruce, if you think I'm going to wander around the streets of Parynko, chasing Martian women, then I'm afraid you're going to be disappointed. If you claim they keep disappearing then I'm willing to take your word for it. But what does it prove?'

By now, Clement was right on the edge of his seat with his eagerness to explain. 'It's simply this. Martians don't in fact exist. The whole population of this wonderful City is one ruddy great hoax. For some reason the City is projecting the presence of inhabitants on to our senses, and we, like the suckers we are, just lap it up. There are all sorts of questions we could ask ourselves about these "Martians", but nobody apart from me has. For instance – why is it that on a planet that is a fraction of the size of Earth the natives are the same stature as us? Why do they look roughly like us? Why are there no graveyards in Parynko? I repeat because there *are* no Martians, the last one died centuries ago. This is just a city of hallucination.'

'But Bruce,' Phil argued, 'what about the people we around us, we hear them, feel them, and can even smell them sometimes?'

'Yes, I know,' agreed Clement, now shifting in his seat. 'The evidence of our own senses is overwhelming, but, and you must believe this, that evidence is wrong. Call it what you will but these people and everything to do with them are just, well, a sort of sensual confidence trick.'

'What about the City, then,' I asked, 'is that non-existent too?'

I'd intended it to be more of a sneer than a question, but Clement treated it as if it were the latter. 'No, I think that is real,' he replied. 'I believe that the City has been left here for a purpose, and that purpose, I think, is being further exploited the longer we stay. As you know, the advances made by our own civilization, in the comparatively short time we've been here, have been nothing short of astounding. No, I think the City is fulfilling its object simply by standing here for the use of any who may find it.'

Apparently, Phil was quite impressed by all this for he asked, 'Bruce, you haven't answered your own questions yet, why *do* the people look like us?'

'Phil, you mustn't get the idea that I know all the answers, I don't. All I have done is to ask the questions. For the rest, I can only guess like yourselves. I suppose an answer to that one is: that the City has made its people in our image, or as near to it as possible. Remember, that a Martian could never, by any stretch of the imagination, be mistaken for a man. They are only human*oid*. I think that *whatever* shape we had been the City would have adjusted its occupants to look as much like us as possible, in order that the first impediment to good relations, alienness, would be minimized. I also think that the atmosphere has been specially prepared and pressurized to suit our metabolism.'

'All right,' I said, 'let us assume for one moment that we *are* going to believe your theory. I personally think it's a load of old moondust, but that's by the way. Just suppose that everything you say *is* so, what then?'

'At the moment,' Clement replied enthusiastically, 'I'm exploring the consequences of my latest idea. If you remember, I said the Martians stay in view so long as they know you're watching them. That, I think, must be the reason Disodo and his family lasted so long. Once Disodo had gone, and I didn't have as much contact with the rest of his family, it didn't take long for them all to follow him.

'So what I'm doing now, is living with another family. I've moved right in, gone native entirely. I share their food, their habits and all their ways. As far as possible I have tried to become a Martian, so as to get them used to me and put them off their guard. Eventually, I'm sure the secret will come out.'

Phil asked, 'But don't they mind you moving in on them like that?'

Clement thought for a moment before replying. 'No, I don't think so. Not to begin with at least, in fact they seemed quite flattered. But lately, I have noticed they've been slightly agitated, and the general atmosphere does seem a bit chillier. I'm fairly certain it's because my presence is now hindering them. It won't be long, and I'll have forced them into the open.'

A long pause followed this remark: Clement sitting back in his chair as if awaiting further questions, Phil apparently kicking the idea over in his brain, and I was toying with the implausibilities of the whole affair.

Eventually I said: 'Bruce, I'm sorry, but as far as I'm concerned, your idea just will not wash. I'm basically practical-minded and therefore I'm not really the best person to try and convince of a rather far-fetched idea.'

'I don't know, Dave,' Phil disagreed, 'I think that Bruce *is* on to something here, but I think that he's letting his imagination have too loose a rein.'

Clement's face became crestfallen and his bearing weary. 'I might have known,' he said, tiredly, 'perhaps I didn't explain it plausibly enough. Still, I've learned my lesson now: I should have kept it to myself. I shan't keep you gentlemen from your leisure any more, I'm sorry I've taken up so much of it already.'

Phil started to say, 'But, Bruce, hold on a –' But Clement stood up, and biting his lower lip, he muttered a barely audible farewell and walked slowly to the door.

When he'd gone I turned to Phil.

'I feel sorry for Clement, you know,' I said, 'although he brings it all on his own head. I suppose I shouldn't have been so frank about it, but don't *you* think that that's the biggest cock-and-bull story you've heard this side of Father Christmas?'

'No Dave, I'm sorry but I don't. I think that basically Bruce Clement has some strong points and the evidence of his own eyes to back them up, but the theory itself is way off-beam. Anyway, let's not argue about it now.' He glanced at his wristwatch. 'If we push along fairly quickly, we might even catch that film yet.'

'Okay,' I replied, 'suits me.'

Phil reached behind him, picked up our caps, tossed mine across to me, and we made our way out into the wide street.

Ahead of us the tall, slightly bent figure of Bruce Clement could be seen quite plainly.

Seeing Clement, Phil remarked, 'You must hand it to Bruce, he sticks to his guns, he must be firmly convinced in his own mind.' We walked in silence for a while, until Phil said suddenly,

'Dave, we've nothing to lose, in fairness to Bruce, let's give his idea a try, after all, we've a good walk in front of us.'

'What do you mean, actually watch to see if one does flit away?' I grinned. 'I think you must have believed him!'

'Yes Dave, let's watch one, that's the only way of satisfying ourselves one way or the other.'

'All right, if you must. We'll watch the same one of course?' Phil nodded. 'How about that one then, the one in the light-blue sash, that's walking close behind Bruce?'

Phil agreed to the choice, and the pair of us kept a fixed stare on the unsuspecting Martian. He was ambling along quite happily, nodding occasionally to passers-by, and generally appeared to be savouring the delights of walking. He wasn't moving quickly, and seemed to be keeping approximately the same relative position to Clement. We followed them thus for about five minutes, and as we were hurrying we had soon almost overhauled them.

Suddenly, with no apparent warning or forethought, the Martian made a smart move to the left, a quick turn of his head – and he was gone. I turned to Phil, my face working as waves of surprise and wonder swept through my mind, 'Phil, did you see that? So quickly!' I stopped at the sight of Phil. He was standing still, his head craning forwards, an expression of utter amazement on his features, still staring unblinkingly up the wide avenue.

'Dave,' he cried simply, 'look!'

I turned and following his gaze, I saw. My heart started pounding inside my rib-cage. Clement's body had twisted agonizingly and seemed to be fighting an inward struggle with itself, as unseen forces pressed him into a kneeling position, his arms flailing, and his tongue crying to the gods for assistance. I made to dash forward but I was too late, he never stood a chance. For with a sudden rush of imploding gases, Bruce Clement disappeared into thinnest air.

And that, give or take a few passages, was the story I told the enquiry tribunal. As far as the Western Nations Space Corps is concerned, Bruce Clement is Missing.

Of course, the enquiry didn't take place all at once, a full-scale search was initiated soon after Masters and myself broke the news, but to no avail. The City was searched, and re-searched, but neither Clement nor his body was discovered. The tribunal was convened, sat, and Phil Masters and I were the chief witnesses. We told all we knew, along with all of Clement's theories. Naturally, the three-man court didn't believe this, and Clement was posted Missing.

Missing. A mystery? Yes, to most of us on Mars, but Phil and I, we *know* the truth. Bruce Clement was taken; snatched by the City of Parynko in order that its secret be left intact. Such was the price of going native, that Clement had to find the truth the only way; the hard way.

But before he went, his knowledge was passed on, and now we, Masters and myself, are the sole guardians of the truth, we *know* the secret of Pary –

Going Native - notes

Then:

Written out of a general wish to be or to become a writer, rather than from the belief that I had something different or individual to say, 'Going Native' was intended as the vehicle for a fairly straightforward science fiction notion. In brief: the Martian city left behind by the last of the people on Mars, discovered millennia later by people from Earth.

Arthur C. Clarke was an influence on me at this time: I always liked his utopian scientific ideas, his belief in the perfectibility of man, the ways in which technology and science could improve the human lot. For me there are distinct echoes in this story of the first novel of Clarke's I ever read, *The City and the Stars*, a book which had had made a deep impression on me as a teenager. For instance, the paragraph beginning, 'The traffic of ground-cars, hovering noiselessly a few centimetres above the ground ...' is clearly an attempt at Clarkean descriptive lyricism. The narrator's description of riding the Belt, which comes near the beginning of the story, also owes a lot to Clarke.

Another influence was John Wyndham. Because I had always enjoyed the way Wyndham's characters had free conversations with each other, I thought his way of telling a story might be my way. For instance, in *The Kraken Wakes* much of the story is reported to the narrator, rather than experienced directly by him. Then there was this sentence from 'Going Native':

> At the time, Phil had in fact been with Arnold's group
> pushing its exploratory way through Syrtis Minor, and
> thus had been spared the brunt of Clement's notions.

Because I could think of no better way of establishing a background I consciously nicked the sentence, or at least its general ambience, from one of Wyndham's books, *The Outward Urge*:

> At that time an exploration party under the leadership
> of Gilbert Troon was cautiously pushing its way up the
> less radioactive parts of Italy, investigating the prospects
> of reclamation.

I thought Wyndham had put it well, and re-used it with the hope no one would notice. No one ever did notice, because out of shyness or nervousness I never submitted 'Going Native' to any editor.

Now:

The sentence structure relies too much on commas, which destroys any sense of rhythm.

There are clear signs of the writer groping for the right words but not finding them. For instance, in the sentence, 'the people of the City go about their business, as far as we can make out, in an uninterrupted fashion' the phrase 'uninterrupted fashion' is clearly the wrong choice.

The relationship between Bruce Clement and Disodo has distinct gay undercurrents, which I now find rather mysterious, and certainly wasn't intended at the time.

The comment about all members of one race looking alike to members of another race – that's also a bit embarrassing.

'Philologists'? Linguists might have been better. I remember being struck by the difficulty people would have when encountering an alien race, culture and language. How would one ever start communicating? I had noticed the ease with which C. S. Lewis 'solved' a similar problem (also on Mars) when he made the central character of *Out of the Silent Planet* into a philologist, who with academic zeal settled down to the task with remarkable effectiveness.

In general, the obvious inexperience shows. The dialogue is structured to talk about plot ideas, with the characters feeding questions to each other. There's a weird semi-military feel to the lifestyle of the people from Earth – the set-up makes me think now of British WW2 films set in RAF bases. The idea for the story isn't a bad one, but so much of it is told by one character to another, rather than depicted graphically or by actions. The descriptions therefore are verbal rather than physical. John Wyndham could do this well, but I was discovering that it's not as easy as it looks.

During the course of my career I have tended to stay away from fiction which is set on other planets or in the far future and this is largely a consequence of the trouble I had with my early work. I was never inspired by the thought of alien worlds, never really believed in them. I felt then, and still feel, that you can get bogged down in descriptions and backgrounds and explanations, and unless you have a particularly fresh imagination or vivid style, you are likely to run into the prosaic stuff that makes 'Going Native' a bit of a challenge to read.

A few years later, my novel *The Space Machine* took the reader to Mars for a series of adventures. That novel is my one foray into the scientific romance, a form more or less invented by the great H. G. Wells. My novel was intended as a kind of homage to Wells, and so all the space travel in that book, all the planetary adventures, were in a kind of self-contained reference to him. Everything was in quotation marks, in a sense. In 1963, that level of relative sophistication was beyond me. I was trying to believe in that stuff.

Stranglehold

(March 1964)

The ship landed on time, a remote speck of light descending swiftly from the cloudy skies above the bleak splendour of a Scottish glen. Its one passenger was met punctually, and Transforred swiftly to London, where the appointment had been made. He travelled by a well-tried route and it was only a few minutes after landing that he emerged from the disguised Transfor into the spring sunshine of suburban Hampstead. The car was waiting, its engine ticking over smoothly and quietly, the smartly dressed chauffeur at the door.

However, the afternoon traffic in Central London was heavy, causing a three-mile traffic jam in the West End, and so, even after the immaculate preparations for fast transit, the visitor was made late for his appointment.

Gasken glanced at his watch for the tenth time in as many minutes, and looked nervously out of the window again. He's never this late, he told himself, there must be a delay, a snag, perhaps a message. In an attempt to occupy his mind he walked over to the mirror on the far wall, and checked that his appearance was right. He adjusted his neat bow-tie by a minute fraction, shuffled his breast-pocket handkerchief, and checked that his hair was unruffled.

His toilet complete he stared blankly at the reflection of his lined face, until, as if drawn by an unseen magnet, he found himself moving towards the window again, half-believing that the act of watching would resolve the impending arrival. He gazed over the long line of parked cars, towards the gates of the factory. The traffic pouring past the entrance was heavy, and it was difficult to identify individual vehicles. After a couple of minutes' watching his eyes started to water, and he blinked several times, clearing his vision.

The tiny hope that the visit might be postponed, his sole consolation, was suddenly crushed. For his anxious eyes now picked out the very lines of the vehicle they were hoping never to see again; the imperturbable high-class modesty of the ever-familiar Rolls-Royce. Its trafficator winking in subdued brilliance the long grey machine left the main stream of traffic and turned sedately past the saluting gatekeeper, and into the grounds of the factory. It stopped in the allotted parking space immediately beneath Gasken's window.

As the driver's door swung smartly open, Gasken moved back from the window, anxious to delay seeing his visitor for as long as possible. He sank heavily into his leather chair behind the desk, and with shaking hands fumbled with a box of pills. Realizing that tranquillizers were useless against the Probe, he finally closed the drawer and attempted to compose himself.

An interminable delay, accentuated by the air-conditioned silence of the expensively decorated office. This was the worst part, he thought in a curiously objective way, the waiting and anticipation.

The taut silence was suddenly broken as the inter-office communicator buzzed loudly. Now that the moment had come Gasken felt better, and it was an almost steady hand that stretched across the deck and depressed a tiny black lever on the receiver.

'Yes, what is it?'

'Mr Arkow to see you,' his secretary in the outer office told him, 'he had an appointment at four o'clock.'

'Thank you, kindly show him in.'

He released the lever and sat back, his hands clasped together. Almost at once the door opened and his secretary came in, preceding the short, darkly dressed figure of his visitor. Fighting down a sudden feeling of dread Gasken rose and extended his hand, smiling cordially.

His secretary said simply, 'Mr Arkow,' and turned to leave. She was just closing the door as Gasken called her back,

'I don't wish to be disturbed for the next couple of hours, please arrange for no phone calls to come through. Oh, and you can go home when you're ready, I won't be needing you any more today.'

'Yes, Mr Gasken.' She left, and shut the door behind her with a muffled click.

The two men faced each other across the desk. Arkow's eyes were calm and disturbing, looking implacably towards Gasken out of a composed face. His features were heavy, his face was round and smooth, curiously lop-sided. Gasken's expression was also still, but motionless with the grip of inner determination and self-control. At all costs he had to appear unruffled, to break down would be fatal. At last, Arkow broke the silence, speaking with the faultless English that unerringly indicates foreign origins.

'Good afternoon to you, Mr Gasken, I trust you are well. I have been concerned for your health recently, both physical and mental, and it was with this view in mind that I arranged this meeting.'

'I'm quite fit Arkow, get to the point, I've no wish that this interview be prolonged unnecessarily.' With his right foot he reached under the desk and gently depressed the pedal switch. A slight click transmitted its motion to him through his foot, and mentally he relaxed a little. He'd get this conversation recorded if it killed him.

Arkow fumbled in his black attaché case. 'I've no doubt,' he said, 'that you are in perfect physical condition, this is no concern of mine. The purpose of my visit, as you are doubtless now aware, is to satisfy myself that our little – experiment – is still working.' He found what he was searching for in his attache case and placed it gently on the desk between them.

The Probe. Gasken recoiled mentally, but with an effort kept his facial expressions controlled.

'But before I conduct my tests,' Arkow continued, 'I want to ask you a few questions.'

Gasken swallowed. At last his control broke, and his face

whitened, and narrowed into a self-defensive frown. It was coming, the mental schizophrenia and frustration of word blocks; the speechless screaming that he dreaded and hated so much. Wordlessly he nodded. Self control was useless, he realized, it always had been. A calm expression had no effect on this –

Arkow flipped down the lid of his case, secured it with the clips and placed the case on the floor. He looked at Gasken, straight in the eyes. 'Mr Gasken, I want you to tell me, in your own words, exactly who you think I am.'

That first question, always the same one, demanding the inevitable answer each time, the same words and intonations that blurted from his lips with the idiot repetition of a faulty gramophone record. His brain fought for a way to avoid saying the words, to speak aloud what he knew in his heart was the truth. Mental pictures formed themselves end hung tantalizingly before his eyes. A loud voice seemed to bellow at his inner ear, subsonically throbbing the words to his vocal cords. His whole frame was alive to the truth. *Arkow is an alien; he must be destroyed; otherwise he will destroy us all; he and his kind are intent on sociological strangulation; economic instability; technological stagnation; he must be destroyed; he must –*

The mental pictures flickered and faded, the subsonics dissipated, and Gasken's tongue started to move easily, flowing with the childish facility of a maniac mnemonic word-wheel. 'You're an old business acquaintance, been dealing with you for years.'

'Excellent, Mr. Gasken, and what is the purpose of my visit?'

Again the mental images, and the shouting and booming of imagined subsonics. *Arkow is an alien; he is here to destroy; strangulation; he must be dest –*

Once more the word block fell into place like a tide gate, and the remorseless churning out of meaningless and automatic syllables. 'We've met to discuss production figures.'

Arkow nodded. 'And finally, what are our present aims?'

Before the mental pictures could form, Gasken's tongue was

moving again. 'We're producing the highest quality article for the lowest possible price, ensuring that our product is wanted by and available to all.'

He stopped and mentally cursed himself for sounding like a second-rate television advertisement. Still, they were Arkow's words and not his own, so there was an excuse. Almost immediately his eyes took on a more normal lustre, 'Does that satisfy you Arkow? Do you want to ask more questions? Go on, I know all the answers, I should do!'

'Yes, you do seem to know the answers, I am eternally impressed at your command of the situation you're in. However,' he shook his round head slowly, 'I must use the Probe.'

Gasken began to speak, but he was too slow, Arkow's hand had leaped out and punched the sensitive plate on the side of the Probe. Gasken's mind wheeled in a sudden flurry of colour, to be instantaneously engulfed in blackness. His body slid noiselessly forward on to the desk.

As Gasken came round to consciousness Arkow was closing his attaché case once more, the Probe was nowhere to be seen. The mists of the artificially induced coma quickly dissipated, and apart from the slightest trace of a headache, left no reaction in his mind. He looked across at Arkow and smiled weakly. 'Well?'

'I'm pleased to tell you that the post-hypnotic suggestions I placed are still intact. A remarkable record! Sixteen years without major renewal. I must commend you on an exceptionally stable mind.'

'No thanks to you Arkow, when will you be finished with me? I can't go on like this much longer.'

The portly alien stood up and walked deliberately to the window. He looked down at the emptying car park with apparent satisfaction. 'You must be patient, when your career as Chairman of this company is finished, then your tasks for us will also be complete. But not before.' He turned to face the back of Gasken's head. 'When are you due to retire?'

'I'll be sixty in two years, I can use my voluntary retirement Pension from then. Needless to say, I will.'

'Mr Gasken, I would remind you that at times I find this task as distasteful as you do. For all our apparent alienness to your life our people are much like yours in many ways, not only in physical appearance. To me this is just another job, at times an unpleasant one, but still a job. I, too, would insist on your retirement in two years. As a person I have formed a great respect for you; it is my one deep regret that we have to behave this way to each other.'

His expressionless face seemed to take on a strange aspect, and for a moment Gasken could have mistaken the face for a human one.

'But let's not talk of irrelevancies,' Arkow suddenly continued, his face an impassive mask once more. 'I would like to see the last quarter's production results.'

Gasken complied wearily. Get it over with for another three months, he thought, another thirteen weeks of enforced silence, unable to speak a word of the truth to anyone. God, how he'd tried! When Arkow had first approached him, on his rise to Chairmanship of the company, his first impulse had been one of horror. He'd tried to kill Arkow then, he recalled, a pity he hadn't succeeded really. Still, there was probably a long line of – his mind stumbled over the word – aliens waiting behind Arkow to take his place, so it wouldn't have had much effect. And then the Probe had appeared; a necessary unpleasantness, Arkow had said at the time, through Gasken's unwillingness to comply. And ever since that black day of enforced will, nothing. His body was totally incapable of even passive resistance.

Gasken was a pawn of Arkow's alien race, an unwitting conspirer against the human race. He'd risen to the seat of Chairman at a comparatively early age, through the nervous collapse of his predecessor, and had met Arkow on his first day in that position. He had been told from the outset about the plan of the aliens, told about the seventy-five years since their machine had been 'invented' and how it had been steadily and insidiously eating its way into civilization. The aliens weren't in a hurry, why should they be, with a lifespan many times that of humans they could afford to wait. Wait while their machines steadily brought a civilization to its knees, whilst appearing to foster it.

Gasken had had to acknowledge the cunning of the plan, the development of a revolution in engineering which applied to industry had in turn revolutionized that. Magnificent technological and sociological achievements made possible by the machine, the face of the planet altered by it; but all the while it was slowly bringing about the strangulation of the very civilization it had helped create.

On that first day, after the Probe had been used with all its mute consequences, Arkow had relaxed a little and told Gasken, in slightly deprecating terms, of the leaders of his race who had devoted the early part of their lives to the 'invention' of this machine. He'd spoken in glowing terms of Hammle, Deezle and Benns, their work on Earth now done, and in famous retirement on their own planet; and told Gasken how, by widespread use of the Probe, they had managed to boost production from a faltering dozen per year, to the thousands now produced every week. With factories all over the world there seemed no stopping the tidal flow of metal.

As he withdrew the file from the cabinet, Gasken was thinking along these lines. This is my contribution to the flow, he thought grimly and wearily, another ten thousand drops in an ocean of metal.

He returned to the desk and laid the file open in front of him. Even as he opened his mouth to speak he felt his mind forcing an optimistic tone. 'We've had some good results this time,' he said helplessly, 'although there was a bit of trouble over redundancy. That installation of machinery you advised last time resulted in two hundred men being laid off, and that brought all the usual trouble with the unions. However, orders have been pouring in, especially from abroad, and we ended the quarter with production seven and three-quarters per cent up on the previous three months.'

Arkow nodded slowly and silently. 'Very good, and development?'

'We're introducing the new range in the autumn, which are almost certain to be big sellers, so I think we need have no fears about the usual winter lapse in sales. Also, this range will be the first to feature those – innovations – you suggested on your last visit. These, I feel, will be very popular.'

'They should be, they were designed so.'

Gasken bit his lower lip, he was hating this. The interview did not last long, Arkow asking the usual questions about production, and Gasken answering almost automatically.

At last Arkow stood up, suddenly and without warning. He extended his hand to Gasken, and bade him farewell, but Gasken did not move. He gazed levelly at Arkow and said, 'To the next time then, and may it be the last.' The alien returned the stare for long moments, turned wordlessly, and walked into the deserted outer offices. As the door swung shut Gasken could hear the racket from the adjoining factory working overtime, as the continuous production line turned out its mass-produced machinery.

He rose, and looked out of the window. The car park was nearly empty now, the majority of the office workers having left for their suburban dormitory-town homes. The immaculate grey Rolls-Royce was still there, its driver leaning casually on the long bonnet. As Gasken watched the chauffeur sprang to attention, and Arkow climbed expressionlessly into the rear passenger seat. After a moment the huge car glided smoothly forwards and made for the exit, where, after a few moments' patient wait, it filtered into the flowing river of traffic, to be borne by it, like flotsam, into the heart of London.

Gasken waited until the car was out of sight, then returned to his desk and slumped across it, his head in his arms. After several minutes he moved as memory came to him. With his foot he searched beneath his desk for the pedal to the recorder. If only the microphone had picked up all that, then the recorder could speak of Arkow, even if he himself were incapable of – He stopped. His questing foot had kicked and cleared the place where the switch had been hidden. In sudden desperation he craned his neck and sought with his eyes for the switch, but it was useless. The pedal switch had been discovered, and taken.

His last hope gone, Gasken fell once more across the desk, but this time his body shuddered as great racking sobs tore at his being, weeping in pitiful desperation for mankind.

The spaceship was several hours late lifting off from the Scottish glen. Its single passenger had been delayed; held up for hours in the off-peak traffic jams of Central London.

Stranglehold - notes

Then:

With this, my second story, I was already beginning to sense that SF could and perhaps should be used for social or political satire. I was influenced by Kingsley Amis, whose 1960 book *New Maps of Hell* had argued strongly for the satirical model. Amis admired writers like Sheckley and Vonnegut, and I did too. I had also been impressed by Cyril Connolly's assertion in *Enemies of Promise* that the use of satire was the one imperative for every writer – it seemed like a tall order for one who was having problems getting sentences finished, but I was game for the challenge.

By this time I had bought my own car and I spent much time driving around the country. It was being borne in on me that the vast numbers of cars and trucks were doing serious, visible and probably irreversible damage to our towns and countryside. However, I was acutely aware of the addictive nature of owning and driving a car, mainly because I shared the addiction. I developed a taste for driving, but it also struck me it might be a plot, with aliens feeding our addiction so as to bring down civilization.

The set-up of a businessman in his office was clearly a hangover from my years auditing the corridors of power. Also clear is the fact that I didn't observe it all that well.

'Gasken' was a made-up surname, based partly on a bit of a car engine called a 'gasket' (whatever I thought at the time that might be), and partly on 'Gaskell', the name of someone I knew. 'Arkow' was the name of a building contractor I saw on the side of a truck. 'Hammle', 'Deezle' and 'Benns' were the result of a clumsy and obscure attempt to disguise the real identities of Hammel (the name of the Dane who built one of the first working automobiles), Diesel (inventor of the compression ignition engine) and Benz (the internal combustion engine). Ouch.

Now:

There are still too many sentences joined up with commas. Many instances of this, but for instance when Gasken says, 'I'm quite fit Arkow, get to the point, I've no wish that this interview be prolonged unnecessarily' it all comes out in a rush, without dramatic or plausible emphasis. Bad punctuation affects all prose, but it's especially true in dialogue.

I did learn from this. Somewhere along the line I discovered that if you read fiction out loud in draft, even just to yourself, you learn about narrative cadence: sentence rhythm, the way words sound in the context of each other, the timing of syllables, paragraph size, the use of pauses, silence.

Dialogue in fiction is an artifice – it does not, should not, attempt to capture the real sounds of real conversations. Anyone who has tape-recorded an interview and then had to transcribe it soon finds that even articulate and thoughtful people tend to speak in an unpunctuated, unstructured gabble of words. Sentences go unfinished, thoughts are not pursued, words are used incorrectly or repeated too often. (And never mind the plethora of 'um's and 'er's.) So when you write dialogue for your characters, and wish to achieve a real-seeming effect, you have to learn verisimilitude: that which seems real but probably isn't. Dialogue should not attempt to capture what was really said, nor even what was supposed to have been said, but should convince the reader that it might have been what was said.

Of course, some novelists or story writers use dialogue in a different way. Some will use it for didactic purposes, or to state views of some kind, and so do not aim to achieve verisimilitude. Each to his own. In this, as in so much of writing, there are no absolutes, no rules.

The point here is that in the stories in this book – and to a large extent in what I write now – I am seeking verisimilitude in dialogue, and so it is by that intent that the result should be judged. Things didn't look too good at this stage, but they did start to improve later.

On this subject, the chit-chat with the secretary is unoriginal and unconvincing, and therefore probably unnecessary.

The relationship between Arkow and Gasken again has the shadow of WW2 hanging over it. A lot of Arkow's dialogue is of the 'good Nazi' kind, who inflicts torture and atrocity with more sorrow than conviction, and tries to make his victim like him for it.

The word 'dissipated' is used twice, both times incorrectly. 'Dissipated' means wasted, scattered or exhausted, or even in a personal sense debauched. 'Evaporated' would have been better the first time, 'dispersed' the second time.

'Artificially induced coma.' – Not a coma. 'Trance' might have been better.

The wrong use of words is always a bit embarrassing, but it often arises, by a sort of paradox, in the work of writers who have spent too much time reading fiction. They pick up an extensive working vocabulary, which is all to the good, but they also tend to make assumptions from context about the meanings of words. More often than not they are right, but it makes them vulnerable to blunders. I still wince at the memory of the time I was rebuked by an editor for using the word 'enervate' to mean 'stimulate' or 'provoke', when it means more or less the exact opposite.

Another sign of people who spend too much time in books is that they have unexpected blind spots about pronunciation. One of the most common mistakes of this kind is pronouncing the word 'misled' to rhyme with 'drizzled'. An early blind spot of my own was a word I always pronounced as 'horry-zon'. I knew perfectly well what it meant, because I had frequently come across it in books. Other people looked out to sea and saw the 'hor-eye-zon'. The moment of realization that they were the same word still lives with me. This is one of the reasons I almost never use the word 'orison'.

The passage which starts with the words 'Gasken was a pawn of Arkow's alien race' is apparently meant as exposition, to convey to the reader what the story was all about. The trouble is that it shrinks from being specific, presumably intending that the reader will work out what's meant by picking up a few hints. As a consequence the passage is too vague for its own good. The art of dribbling out background information, without being either too secretive or too expository is something that can only be acquired by practice.

This sort of problem is not unique to SF or other kinds of fantastic literature. Historical novelists have a similar task to perform, for instance. The problem can be illustrated by the opposite.

If I write a story set in present-day London, I need only a few words to convey the background: the tube trains, the Thames, the towers of Canary Wharf, etc. Similarly, blow a tumbleweed across the drifting sand outside a roadhouse and play a Patsy Cline record, and you're on a back highway in America's West. Describe someone with his collar turned up lighting a cigarette in a dark alley next to a rain-wet cobbled street, and the scene is set for a thriller.

But in a story like *Stranglehold*, where the era might or might not be the present day, where society could have small differences from our own, where social mores or nuances could have different layers of meaning, where technology might be superior to our own, then the information has to be given to the reader, or at least suggested.

'The new range in the autumn, which are almost certain.' – Collective noun, singular verb.

Who the devil were 'Hammle, Deezle and Benns'?

Star Child

(NOVEMBER 1964)

The old man's arm swung, and the tiny fish described a graceful, fluttering arc through the golden summer sky. Dazzling and silver, it plunged neatly into the water. Lazily the ripples spread, losing themselves in the miniature swamp of the reed-lined bank. Overhead a swallow dipped and shot away, taking its claimed prize from the cloud of insects flying by the further bank.

The old man stared meditatively at the dying ripples, and finding some connection, looked sideways at the Child on his left. Just as the water shows effect of impact, so humanity leaves ripples in its wake. A minor upheaval and a reshaping in life, and the spread of change flows remorselessly through the world. The analogy ends here though, water rediscovers its original balance, humanity does not.

He stirred himself, and wound in the hook for rebaiting.

'Child,' he said, for he knew no other name for his small companion. 'Child, you and I are living in a world like none other men have known. I have lived in two worlds, one good and one bad. One has had the hope of everlasting refinement; one has been doomed to failure. One was a gay and happy world; the other a place of lost understanding and pitiful woe.

'Now, both worlds are to end. Mine has gone already, and yours is to join it. My life will soon be over and when I die, both of my worlds will go to the grave with me.'

The Child, not understanding, fidgeted and watched with innocent blue eyes the old man's fingers singing deftly as they replaced the bait. With a flick of the wrist, the line was cast into the pool, and as the float steadied, the old man relaxed once more.

'All the wonders you Children have missed, all the beauties and all the joys. How can I tell you so you'd understand? I am alone in a world that is no longer my own. Mine has gone, swept away by something that I can't even pretend to understand.'

The Child stared mutely up at the man. The transparent expression covered an animal mind, a cunning and immature slyness that marked him down as typical of his race.

His back was aching so the old man lay right back, his hands clasped loosely across his stomach. He gazed up into the boundless haze of sky, thinking of his past. Soon he began to talk of the old days, knowing only too well that his words fell on deaf ears. Pushed by a sudden wave of nostalgic longing he spoke automatically and uncaringly – the Child wasn't listening, but these were words for the whole universe to hear. Not just a single uninterested Child.

I was the first person (the old man said) to get to the moon. Come to think of it, I'm probably the last as well. I was blasted off from Florida like the cog in the machine I was. There was no personal glory in my flight, it was the outcome of many years' hard work and research by a team – nothing more. This team was punching rockets into the sky while I was still at college, and by the time I enrolled with NASA, they were old hands at the game. In fact, when the time came, it was just like another bout of training. Not a single technical foul-up all the way.

As soon as the acceleration had finished, and the ship was safely in free-fall, I hitched myself up in my impact-couch and looked through the rear port. There it was, just as my space-experienced colleagues had described it to me, the most beautiful sight in the universe. Earth. The radio was clamouring, partly from static, and partly from urgent queries from Control. Reluctantly I made my reports, not wishing to tear myself away from the view, until finally I was able to settle back for the four-day flight in free-fall.

And then, at this very moment of relaxation, I saw it. My first impression, one of a huge darkness, was caused by the shadow. Suddenly the sun appeared to go out, as the capsule's ports lost their sun-halation, and the gentle whine of the solar generators sank slowly into silence. I pulled myself to the port as cautiously as I could – and saw it. A huge ship, large beyond description. Painted in gold and black stripes, bulbous, grotesque and unutterably alien. From a mile-long battery of exhaust venturi, the blue wash of ion-plasm pointed a stabbing finger at the northern Asiatic continent. It took a whole minute for the ship to pass me, even with our differences in relative speeds. The last I saw of the ship it was still sinking, dropping away into the atmosphere.

I switched on the headset and called Control. I told them what I'd seen, and where I thought it was going to land. Control was halfway through its reply when the radio shut off with a note of finality that shook me. I didn't hear from Earth for the rest of the trip. Nor ever again.

The rest of the flight was the most terrifying experience of my life. I landed without mishap on the very face of the moon, in the Mare Nubium. While I was there, I was supposed to leave my capsule and make the obligatory first steps on the moon. Such was the effect of this enforced radio silence on me, however, that I could not bring myself to open the hatch. After an hour's deliberation, I returned to my couch and punched the pattern for my homeward flight.

It wasn't that I had lost the urge for adventure, it was just a plain simple desire to go home. Every hour, on the flight back, I called up Control with no success – only the random muted roar of static met my ears. As time passed I grew more and more depressed, especially as I could see the shining blue orb of Earth hovering in front of my forward port.

Then it happened again. I was getting ready to start my re-entry pattern, when an ominous shadow fell across my port. This time I was prepared for what I was going to see. Our orbits were more coincidental, and I got a long, long look at the departing intruder. The mammoth ship was accelerating hard, the ion-plasma exhaust amplified by the shrill white torch of nuclear reaction. Fascinated, I stared with mixed feelings of horror and wonder. Great streamers of light were flowing from ports and nozzles, long trailers of some metallic substance were spread behind, and the whole machine was rotating slowly, its black-and-gold finish reflecting the light of the sun erratically. The last I saw of it was as it disappeared from sight in the general direction of the Orion constellation, its mysterious errand on Earth complete. Once more I tried to raise Control, this time in desperation, but all I got was the now-familiar silence. I was lying with tears in my eyes as the first shock of the retro-rockets slammed me into the depths of my impact-couch. As the black depths of unconsciousness claimed me, a feeling of stark loneliness washed over me.

I awoke to a sound I had been trained to listen for, yet it was a sound I had never in fact heard. Maybe it is the song of the astronauts' guardian angel, but the sound of cool air rushing through the wispy metallic parachute did little to comfort me. I lay there for many hours it seemed, before I hit the sea. As soon as I was sure we had hit, I fired the escape-hatch, and fought my way out.

I slithered clumsily down into the water, and struck out for the nearest of the waiting ships. Just as planned, the capsule had re-entered into the Caribbean, dead on target. I swam several hundred yards in my clumsy spacesuit, before pausing for breath. Just as I had feared, there was no sign of life on board the ship, just a thudding silence. From where I was floating I could see the name, the *U.S.S. Sacramento*. On her after-deck was a bright-red painted 'copter, a cheering sight, because I had learned to fly one in my training.

I swam hard to the ship, my muscles exulting in the exercise, after so long without movement. I was climbing clumsily up the Jacob's Ladder as I heard a loud sucking noise from behind me. Turning, I saw my capsule sinking fast, belching and groaning as the water poured in over her valuable instruments. Quickly and without fuss she disappeared, leaving a sad and empty place in my heart; I felt as if a part of my life had drowned with her.

I came out amidships. The overall silence had made me think that I was alone in the world, but now I found I was wrong. The *Sacramento* had her full crew all right, but as far as I could tell, every individual one of them was babbling insane.

All around me they lay. Officers and men, young and old, all were on the deck, their eyes staring outward, not focusing. Most of them had clamped their teeth on their tongues, and all were wounded in some way. One man had shot his own throat out, and another had cut his wrists on the rusty wire holding the bridge awning. As I walked unsteadily around the ship I saw more and more bodies, all of them heinous suicides. Those still alive were beyond recall, their idiot faces blank and lifeless. I had nearly reached the 'copter when a young rating charged from nowhere, straight at me. His eyes were rolling, his cheeks flecked with foam, and in his hand he was carrying a vicious-looking knife. He swung at me hard, going for my throat, but fortunately his aim was wild and high. I was able to floor him with little trouble, and he lay where he fell, muttering incoherent curses and inaudible sentences. Soon, he became silent, and I left him.

Shaking, I wriggled into the pilot's seat in the 'copter.

The old man had turned on his side, away from the Child, the memory of that awful day clouding his eyes and dimming his vision. He sobbed silently for a while.

'I flew back to the mainland,' he said after a long pause, 'and found much the same thing there. As far as I could tell I was the only sane man left alive on Earth. I walked for hours through the remains of civilization, shouting and calling; but no one answered. At last, I found you, a new-born baby then, still attached to your mother by the umbilical cord. I don't know whether it was the strain of your birth, or the sudden madness, but your mother was dead beside you. Your father had shot himself in the same room.'

The Child still said nothing as his fingers strayed restlessly to the tin of ground bait. He picked up a grub, and pulled it apart with obvious delight.

The old man took the remains from him, and threw them into the pool. 'We've lived together for so long,' he said. 'All these years I've looked after you and you still do things like that.'

The Child stared at him with the same innocent expression he always had, and the man was immediately sorry for the reprimand. 'Come on,' he said. 'I've talked long enough. You must be tired.'

They cleared up the litter of the day's fishing, and the old man carefully stowed away his rod and line. Hand-in-hand, they walked away from the clearing and into the forest. The old man stooping, his back trouble giving him pain again, and the Child, stunted and emaciated. But the Child's blue eyes were untroubled under the mat of grey hair, and his mouth was set firmly beneath his beard.

Together they walked back to the cave, through the empty world.

Star Child - notes

Then:

It might seem a remarkable thing, but I have absolutely no memory of writing this story – I no longer know what inspired it, what I thought it would turn out to be, even what sparked it off.

Written in 1964, it pre-dates the first NASA moon landing by five years, and even pre-dates the preparatory Apollo missions. I have never had a technical ability with describing machines, spaceships, and so on, and this story is full of fairly obvious avoidance of that kind of thing. With hindsight, anyone who has seen NASA broadcasts can fill in the technical gaps of the actual flights to and from the moon (which would amount to about 99% of what's not in the story, at a conservative estimate), but omissions seem to be most of what's wrong with the descriptions.

I have said many times that I never write stories about spaceships and spacemen. I really had forgotten this one.

The story is similar in tone to Brian Aldiss's *Greybeard*, published in the same year. I think I might have read Aldiss's novel before I wrote this, but I can't be sure any more. Shades of John Wyndham's *The Midwich Cuckoos* too, with its visiting starship doing quietly mysterious things. It also has some similarity to the movie *Independence Day*, but as that wasn't released until 1996 I'm fairly sure I hadn't seen that at the time.

Now:

'Star Child' is another story told by one character to another, so the reader is distanced by one step from the narrative. It raises the familiar question that is raised by any story told within a frame: why now? Why has the character never told his story before this moment?

The 'framing' device is still useful as a technique in fiction, and still used, but it seems slightly antique these days. I first realized this a few years after writing 'Star Child', when I became interested in the writings of H. G. Wells.

Most of Wells's best work was produced in the first ten years of his career, roughly from 1895 to 1905 – the Wells books most people have read and enjoyed and can remember by title were written in that period. Also, most of his best short stories. Of those, a large number were told through a 'frame': a mariner's yarn, a story narrated in a bar, and so on. One of his best-known books, *The Time Machine*, is in formal terms almost a template for this kind of thing: the book opens and closes with an after-dinner conversation, during which the main story is told to the assembled listeners. Another famous example of a frame novel is Mary Shelley's *Frankenstein*, which is a series of found letters and told narratives, some of them nested within others.

My Wellsian homage, *The Space Machine*, makes no gesture towards this: the reader is thrown into the action and direct narrative from the first page. That seemed to me the best way of telling the story, but about halfway through writing it I did briefly wonder if that break with the form was a break too far. Maybe *The Space Machine* too should be presented as a manuscript found in an archive, a recapitulation of an old story, a collection of papers found in a family desk? When I came to think about it like that it all seemed a bit much, and I left my novel as it was. But our habitual dispensing with the 'frame' indicates, I think, a universal familiarity with the idea of fiction. Modern readers do not expect to have the inventiveness of the story broken to them gradually, distanced from themselves and the writer by having an intervening narrator.

It was this wish for a distance, a shelving or sharing of responsibility, that lay behind the way I told 'Star Child.' I can't see now a better way of doing it, but I think that is caused by the thinness of the material in the story.

The sentence structure is better for the most part. The sentences are shorter, and have fewer dependent clauses. But there's this from the second paragraph: 'The analogy ends here though, water rediscovers its original balance, humanity does not.'

'A vicious-looking knife'? Is there any other kind? Philip Pullman invented a subtle knife, but the rest seem pretty aggressive to me.

If the Child has 'a mat of grey hair', and has a beard, how old then must the narrator be? We know he must be much older, but this twist at the end risks implausibility.

The Witch-Burners

(JANUARY 1965)

The stars were shining that night, as he took his last walk. His way lay down quiet lanes and leafy paths, through the old and straggling wood. He'd played here many times as a child, and even the passage of twenty years hadn't changed things much.

There was a gentle breeze blowing, carrying the fresh, new smell of greenwood. He breathed deeply, knowing that tomorrow he would savour this brief escape like no other time in his life. He shut his mind to these thoughts, in surroundings like these images of death seemed alien and foul.

The path began to widen, and the trees grew more sparsely; soon he came to the glade he knew so well. In the centre was the old tree stump.

He sat there for a long time. Thinking the old thoughts, the ones he'd tried to express so often, and yet had failed somehow to translate into a conviction he could express verbally. He knew he was right, if only he could convince the rest of the world.

He looked up at the night sky. The stars were bright and clear, seeming to shun him with their own indifference. How ironical, he thought. I am the one who could show mankind the way to the stars, and yet I am hunted like an animal for that very reason. He clenched his fist. Strength, he said to himself, if only I could fight against them. Show them the truth. His face dropped into his hands and he sat there for a long time. Listening to the sounds of the forest, the wind in the trees, the leaves brushing against themselves – smelling the sweet odours of raw, unharmed life. Feeling the goodness of life, yet ever-conscious of the tightening net of evil.

Perhaps he could run. They wouldn't be here until the morning, that would give him several hours' start. But ... The optimism faded as quickly as it had come. His face was too well known. He could never hope for a safe hiding place.

No, it would be better to shorten the agony, meet his fate here in the forest of his childhood memories. Better to die at home, than live in strangeness and fear.

'John Gregory,' a voice said. A strange and tuneful voice; one like he'd never heard before. His train of thought was broken, suddenly his mind filled with relief and relaxation. All at once, he had no cares, his worries wore blown away on the breeze and he himself like a normal human being once again.

But it was only a temporary respite. With chilling speed his depression returned to him. Then, he felt a hand on his shoulder.

'Gregory,' the voice said. 'Look at me.'

The man raised his head. Although it was dark in the glade, he could see who had spoken to him. It was a youth, thin and slight, a person of incredible frailty.

'Do not be scared of me,' the youth said. 'I am your only friend.'

Gregory looked again, saw an expression of extreme compassion, saw a youthful face with the softening lines of mature experience.

'Who are you?' he said.

'My name is Torla,' the youth replied. 'As I said, I am now your only friend. I have travelled for many thousands of miles to help you.'

'You're too late. Nobody can help now.'

Gregory looked more closely at this youth, who had called himself Torla. His clothes were strange. He wore a simple wrap and tunic, in plain grey colour. By the light of the stars, Gregory could see that his skin was a deathly white, and his eyes a deep black.

'Where do you come from?' he said.

The youth frowned, and turned away. 'I would tell you fully,' he said, 'but you would have difficulty in comprehending. You see, I come from the stars; I belong to a race of space dwellers who are the rulers of this sector of the galaxy. Had you, John Gregory, been allowed to develop your star-drive, we are the first race you would have discovered.'

Gregory, a dreamer all his life, stared at the young man. At another time or in another place, he would have laughed out loud at what he'd just heard. But now, at the emotional and physical climax of his life, he saw and believed. Beyond the young man, Gregory suddenly saw a piece of metal, glinting faintly in the starlight.

The youth saw Gregory's eyes move, and followed his gaze. 'My craft,' he explained simply.

Gregory turned away from the youth and crossed to the edge of the glade. He leaned against a tree, staring at the ground, not looking towards the young man. Many long minutes passed before he looked back at Torla. He was still standing where he'd been before, waiting patiently.

'You say you can help me?' he said to him at last.

The youth sat down on the edge of the stump. 'You must appreciate,' he said, 'that there is no easy way out. Your race is not yet conditioned to the dream of the stars; mundane and trivial factors rule their thinking.

'You are a rebel, you're ahead of your own time. And although your thinking is thousands of years behind that of my own race, it is so advanced, comparatively, that you must suffer for it.'

Gregory groaned. 'I realize that, but I must research. With this constant hounding, I can't continue my work.'

'I can help you, Gregory. I can definitely help you. But only temporarily. Whatever I do to assist you, will only get you over this present obstacle. You must solve your other problems yourself.'

Gregory stood before the youth, and gazed down at him desperately. 'But why? My work is going to be for the eventual good of the world, yet my only reward is pain and fear. Help me now, and ...'

A flash of anger fled across Torla's face, but faded as soon it as it was born. 'Gregory!' he shouted, then subsided. 'Look at it from our point of view,' he said more rationally. 'Your race is an immature one, as evidenced by its attitude towards your discovery. And yet, it is a potentially powerful and mighty breed, one that could one day rule a Universe. My people are the present rulers of this sector, and yet we are willing to become a subject race in the face of powerful opposition. Your people are possible contenders. I have been sent to Earth to make a decision on this matter. It is the unique maturity of your discovery that has forced this.'

Gregory looked startled. 'But why?'

'It goes back a long way. Almost to the dawn of our own civilization. The only hope that planet-bound man has of spreading through the Universe is with a star-drive such as yours. You don't realize this yet, but ...'

He broke off suddenly, as a faint howling of dogs rose in the distance. Gregory turned sharply, looking in the direction the noise had come.

'They're coming,' he said. 'They've followed my trail.' He grabbed hold of Torla. 'You said you were going to help me!' he shouted, desperation colouring his voice. 'They'll be here in a few moments, what are you going to do?'

'Follow me.' Torla ran off in the direction of his craft, and after a second Gregory followed him. As he got nearer, be could see the size of the machine. It wasn't the conventional rocket shape he'd subconsciously assumed, it was more like an inverted cork. It was smaller than he'd imagined, only a few feet above his own head. By the time he got there, Torla had levered open a hatch, and was reaching inside.

As he arrived, Torla turned to meet him. He was holding an object whose dimensions were hard to estimate in the dimness of the trees. It was at least two feet long, and made of a dark substance, black, or a very deep brown.

Suddenly, the howling of the dogs, that had been getting imperceptibly louder, stopped. A damp silence surrounded them, like a cold and sudden sweat. Gregory tried to slow his gulping breaths, as he strained to hear. Then, he heard barking, gunfire, crashes ... faint noises, yet clear ones.

'They've found my cottage,' he said, as the realization hit him that now he had nowhere to go. That had been his last resort, the cottage hidden away in the woods, his birthplace and home. And now it had gone. He stiffened as the old hatred of unreasoning and illogical action came over him. They'd had no need to wreck his house, they were vandals. The cold sweat that had pervaded the trees, now seemed to spread to him, and he tensed himself against the rage he knew would follow.

Torla seemed to sense this hatred. 'Don't,' he said. 'It had to come sooner or later. If it hadn't happened tonight, they would have looted it tomorrow.'

'My papers, all my notes –'

There was an explosion, and a white glare went up into the sky. Faintly, through the trees, he could hear shouting voices and more barking. The glare deepened into a bright red suffusion of light, highlighted by sparks. He stood there for a minute or so, staring at this glow that was his own funeral pyre. It must have reassured him somehow, for when he turned back to Torla, his eyes seemed oddly resigned, for the glint of loathing had disappeared.

'Show me,' he said. 'As quickly as you can. They'll be here soon. Those animals you can hear will follow my trail.' Even as he spoke, the barking of the dogs died away, to be replaced by the baying and howling of a pack of hounds in chase. A great sense of urgency hit him, suddenly the most important thing to him was to be shown how to use the weapon, then to be left alone.

Torla seemed to read his mind. 'Don't make mistakes, John Gregory. This is no ultimate weapon. It is not a device of force, for my people would have no use for it.' He looked over his shoulder in the direction of the noise. 'No civilized people should have.'

The noise was louder now. Gregory's lifelong habit of a short evening walk had laid its own trap. Over the noise of the hounds, they could hear men's voices, shouting. Through the trees came the first brief glimpse of a flashing torch.

'Quick, man. Show me how to use it, then go!'

'I'll do that. But I must emphasize something. You must not

expect this to fight your battles for you, that you must do yourself. No amount of mechanical display will convince your peoples of the wonder of your invention. This will only enable you to escape tonight, and live in comparative safety in future.'

'Get on with it, for Christ's sake!'

'This will not kill people, it will not even make them submit to your will. It is a machine used extensively in our surgeries, for treating diseases of the brain. Direct the beam at anyone's head, and they will fall into a temporary coma. Remove the beam from them, and they will recover in several minutes.'

'How do you operate it? Hurry man!' Gregory was almost screaming, in his agony of anticipation. The men had reached the far side of the clearing and were beginning to swarm across it. The leading man had two hounds, pulling and straining at their leads.

'It is quite a simple operation. To release the beam, you open this slide – here. You then pull back this lever – here, and –'

'You there. Stop!' A loud and authoritative voice fired through the trees. 'Put your hands on to your heads, both of you!' A brilliant beam of light lanced through the trees and splashed around the two men. Another followed, then another.

Gregory seized the weapon from Torla, and lifted it into what he thought looked like a firing position.

'Get back, all of you!' he shouted. 'I'm armed!' Quietly, he hissed at Torla, 'How's this thing work? Is it loaded?'

'You don't have to load it, what happens ...'

A shot rang into the sky. 'The next one's for you, Gregory! Throw that toy away, and get your hands up.'

The intense white lights were still playing on them. Into the dazzling light, Gregory could see nothing. An idea formed.

'Torla,' he whispered. 'Fire this thing at one of the lights. See if we can show them we're not bluffing.'

He took it, but said, 'I've told you, this is not a weapon.'

'Keep still, Gregory, we don't want to have to shoot you yet!'

Gregory tried to shield the light from his eyes. 'I don't know who you are,' he shouted. 'But I'm warning all of you this thing is a weapon and I mean to use it.'

A quiet voice at his elbow. 'I'm ready, Gregory.' Torla moved quickly. He raised the black object and pointed it at one of the lights. Nothing happened, then a second later the light wavered and the lamp fell to the ground. Its beam lanced up into the air, illuminating the leaves above them.

'What the devil!' The voices around them started shouting. Then a shot roared, and Torla folded quietly into the grass.

'My God!' Gregory looked down at the small body at his feet, almost not believing that it had happened. Slowly, his hands went up above his head.

The men stood around him in the dark, toying impatiently with their weapons. The dogs were gone, their job done. In the distance, the glare from the burning remains of his house was fading fast. A storm was building up, the noises of the forest seeming empty and muffled in the humid still.

The leader of the men, some kind of officer, offered Gregory a cigarette.

'My last one, eh?' Gregory grinned ironically.

'Your last one. What makes you do it? An intelligent man like you should have known a little better than this.'

Gregory thought for a minute. 'I can't explain it to you, you're not a scientist. Until you've ever had the knowledge that what you're doing is right, and is worth fighting for, then no amount of explanation will make it clear.'

'But *are* you right? How can anything so much in contravention of everything that's good be "right"?'

Gregory looked at his interrogator. It was suddenly obvious that here was a man of no small intelligence. He must be almost like himself, fighting for what *he* thought was right. The only trouble was, Gregory reflected ruefully, he was a minority of one, this man had a majority that agreed with him.

'Up until tonight,' he explained, 'I only thought I was right. But now I know, and it is because of him.' He pointed with his glowing cigarette end at the small covered body of Torla, still lying where he had fallen. 'That man, I believe, came from the stars.'

The officer thought about it, then shook his head. 'I don't believe it,' he said flatly.

'Let me finish,' Gregory said. 'Tonight was the first time I ever met that man. He came to me because he knew he had to help me. He landed in that craft,' Gregory indicated the white shape behind him, 'which, as far as I know, could never have been made anywhere on Earth. As proof, he told me that my invention, the very one for which I am about a to die, is the only star-drive that will ever take man to the stars. I can only assume that that craft,' he indicated it again, 'is powered by some adaptation of my principle.'

The officer looked surprised, and a little sick. His attitude of personal friendliness vanished, and the professional, legal killer returned to his face. 'Just as well, then,' he said, 'that we got him too.'

Gregory's cigarette end glowed as he took the last suck on it. He ground it into the soil with his heel. 'I'm ready,' he said quietly.

The officer took his arm, and called his men.'

In the distance, the first rumblings of the coming storm could be heard. They took Gregory out into the glade, and stood him before a tree. The officer tied his arms, spat in his face, and walked away.

At a signal, four rifles fired, and John Gregory died.

They cut him down, and laid his body beside that of his only friend. The officer went into the spacecraft and looked for the drive compartment. It didn't take long to find, there weren't many places to search. There, in the midst of all the wiring and machinery, embedded in its crystal tomb, was the brain of a human being.

They burnt the spacecraft before they left it. They flooded it with petrol, threw the bodies in, tossed a brand in after them, and watched it blaze. Like witch-burners of centuries before, they took a morbid and self-righteous delight in seeing it burn. Then as its remains were smouldering and smoking, they made their way back to the town, marching like victors into Rome. As they went down through the trees, the smoke from the craft joined with the piling clouds in hiding the stars from the face of the Earth.

The Witch-Burners - notes

Then:

A mood piece, trying to wring the heartstrings. Some subjects lend themselves naturally to SF, but some don't. I think this kind of yearning about the futility of science developing too fast is misjudged.

The influences here were the American writers Clifford D. Simak and Fredric Brown.

Simak was an influence because he was enjoying success in the 1960s and there were many of his books around. He wrote a superior form of this kind of thing often and well, and I liked what he did. His stories were full of people hanging around in the woods, or rocking meditatively on the back porch, wondering in simple terms about complicated things, regretting the onrush of technology, and so on.

Brown came into it too because he was a good storyteller who had a journalistic knack of pulling unexpectedly at the reader's emotions. I think I had recently read Brown's novel *Project Jupiter*, which was a huge influence on me at the time I was writing these stories. His work is largely forgotten now, but he wrote three splendid SF novels of their day: *Project Jupiter*, *The Mind Thing* and *What Mad Universe?*. The last of these is *sui generis*, a timeless classic that doesn't show its age, while being at the same time completely and hopelessly out of date. Its wonderful appeal can be summed up by saying that *What Mad Universe?* does for the SF pulp magazines what the film *Galaxy Quest* did for *Star Trek*, and with the same amusement, irreverence, fantastic imagination ... and love.

However, in 1965, although I was aware of most of that, it

would not have been possible for me to articulate it in any way. I just wanted to write the story with the tools and abilities I then had.

As far as I remember, 'The Witch-Burners' was never shown to any professional editor – not a bad thing, I suspect.

Now:

Most of what is wrong is on the first page (but not all, perhaps). For instance, the narrative is written with verb contractions, e.g.: 'He'd played here many times as a child, and even the passage of twenty years hadn't changed things much.'

I have always been undecided about the use of contracted verb-forms in fiction. On the one hand, saying 'I'd' or 'didn't' and any of the others makes the text more colloquial, and therefore more approachable and readable. A lot of American writers use contractions freely, probably for those reasons. 'Write as you speak' is not a bad rule to follow.

But at the same time, perhaps fiction should be seen as an exercise in English, that the full range and beauty of the language should be deployed, without concessions to vernacular English?

As I say, I am undecided. Look again at the sentence I picked out:

> *He'd played here many times as a child, and even the passage of twenty years hadn't changed things much.*

Would that be better as?:

> *He had played here many times as a child, and even the passage of twenty years had not changed things much.*

Sometimes the full form of a verb can make a sentence seem laboured, over-formal, pedantic. No one wants to write like a local government official. At other times, it can make the image stronger, leave no doubt about what the writer is saying. I suppose the answer is one of moderation. If the cadence requires verb contractions, then a writer should feel able to use them. On the other hand, vernacular English is for speaking, not writing. The full form is sometimes better. Think of both.

I suspect the truth is that when I wrote 'The Witch-Burners' I did not (didn't) know the difference, that I was writing by ear in an idiom I was only just beginning to get to grips with.

'Images of death seemed alien and foul.' – Using the word 'seemed' weakens the image. 'Were' would have been better. Even though the character might only be perceiving something in a gradual way, the reader intuitively wants clearer, more immediate descriptions.

'His face dropped into his hands.' – Really?

The arrival of the UFO is a bit fortuitous, opening many questions and answering none of them.

The 'voice' of the story is unconvincing. There is a kind of sobbing dread throughout the story, presumably acquired impressionistically from the feelings of the character. But why should the writer and reader endure the same emotions as the players in the story? A greater distance from the mood would make the story more, not less, moving. We know nothing about the narrator beyond his fears, so have no information by which to judge his present experiences.

I remember that when I finished 'The Witch-Burners' I believed it represented a step forward, that it wasn't too bad, that I should keep on trying.

Impasse

(SEPTEMBER 1965)

The Denebian intruder was dragged before the Field-Marshal.

'We found him skulking around the camp, sir,' the young Lieutenant reported. 'He was armed, and in possession of several documents.'

'I come in peace,' the intruder protested in fluent English. 'Deneb wants a truce.'

The Field-Marshal was a stern, straight-backed man; under a crop of white hair his eyes held a gleam of virility. He leaned forward, and stared intently at the Denebian. 'A truce, heh? Then account for the amassing of your fleet over our planet, the loss of our cruisers last week, and yesterday's crippling attack on Mars. Now you call for truce. You underestimate my intelligence, friend.'

'I credit you for what you have.' The Denebian moved towards the desk, away from the Lieutenant's restraining hold. 'Earthmen are inferior in every way; their culture, their science, and their customs. To us it is like waging a war with animals. For your own good we offer truce.'

'What are the conditions?'

'We ask only one thing: stay in your solar system. Do this, and you will be left in peace. Our battleships will disperse, and your prisoners returned.'

The Field-Marshal threw his swagger-cane on to the desk in disgust. 'Take him away, Lieutenant. How long will it take these stupid apes to realize that they're dealing with human beings! Preposterous!'

The Lieutenant seized one of the intruder's four arms, and pulled him towards the tent-flap.

'Wait.' The Field-Marshal got up from behind his desk. 'Let him go, Lieutenant. I think we'll free him after all.' He looked with evident distaste at the alien. 'You go; and take *my* truce terms with you. Yes. When you get back to your generals, you tell them from me that they can have peace if they like; but on Earth's conditions. Unless I get an undertaking within six Earth hours that the Denebian fleet will never again leave the confines of their home solar system, then my fleet will destroy your planets. That'll sort things out.'

The intruder looked alarmed. 'This is ridiculous. Our ships are poised to strike even now.'

'Mine, my dear Denebian enemy, are similarly poised. In fact, unless I personally countermand a specific order before this evening, my fleet will start its action.'

The Denebian began to look impatient, as if tired of trying to communicate against such inferiority. 'For your information, Field-Marshal, unless I return to our flagship within two Denebian hours, with a signed treaty, of course, then my navy will attack *you.*'

The Field-Marshal unclipped his service automatic. 'There's an easy answer to that problem,' he said.

'Barbarian tactics won't work, either. You see, if I'm killed a relay situated in my adrenalin gland will close, and trigger a biochemical nuclear explosive. In short, to use one of your nauseous expressions, if I go, you go with me.'

'Damned clever, aren't you? Your little zombie brains think of everything, eh? Just let me remind you, that if I don't reverse that order tonight ...'

The Denebian's manner stiffened. 'Release me, please. I see no reason why I should waste my time further.' The Field-Marshal nodded to the Lieutenant, and the intruder was freed. He walked slowly to the flap, and turned.

'I'll wait outside for a few minutes,' he said. 'Then if you change your mind about signing ...' The flap closed, and he disappeared into the bright sunlight.

The Field-Marshal looked at the Lieutenant. 'Bluffing?'

The Lieutenant nodded slowly. 'In my experience, sir, the Denebians don't have sufficient intelligence to strategize a boxing match, let alone an interstellar war. They're animals.'

The supreme Field-Marshal of the Earth forces chuckled. 'You're so right,' he said. He retrieved his swagger-cane from the desk, checked the magazine of his automatic, and went outside and shot the Denebian.

Impasse - notes

Then:

'I should keep on trying' – see my final comment on 'The Witch-Burners', above. Perhaps anyone reading 'Impasse' might wonder what I thought I was trying to do that was worth keeping on.

Another story lies between the two stories: 'The Run', which became my first-sold story and which has been left out of this collection for that reason.

At the time of writing 'Impasse', such a very short story, my burning ambition to write and sell fiction was as bright as ever, but I was constantly short of ideas that I felt were strong enough. A story like 'Impasse' helped stop the gap, because it was a riddle story, a one-liner, something I could craft into shape quickly and well enough.

It was the second story I sold to Kyril Bonfiglioli. ('The Run' was published in May 1966.) 'Impasse' appeared in the February 1967 edition of *SF Impulse*, some eighteen months after I had sent it in. Bon ran an art gallery in Oxford, editing the magazine on the side. As I described earlier, submitting a manuscript to inertia-prone Bon was as good a way as any one might devise of losing sight of it forever, so he tended to have stories offered to him after everyone else had rejected them.

This was not the case with 'Impasse' – I could not think of anyone else who would dream of publishing it, so Bon received it first. It eventually crawled out of his wormhole not long before he resigned from the editorship. The little blurb at the top of the story complimented me on my mordant wit.

I don't recall any comments on the story when it appeared in the magazine, and it has never been reprinted until its inclusion here.

Now:

The best thing about the story is that it's short.

It depends on simple, stock SF words, ideas and vocabulary: 'Denebian', 'Earthmen', 'interstellar war', etc., so there's no possibility of it transcending its own genre.

The brisk style and narration is good enough.

The SF world has a likeable tradition of publishing very short stories – that is, fiction that does not exceed about 1,000 words. They generally depend on a twist or surprise ending, and are known as 'vignettes', although this use of the word seems to have originated in the American science fiction magazines and perhaps other genres. In general publishing circles, a vignette (which is derived from a French word meaning 'little vine') is either a floral decoration at the front of a book, or it means a short literary essay, one which describes someone's character. A vignette is also a photographic process, in which the edges of a print are graduated to create an oval or circular effect around the subject. For this pedantic reason, I have always tried to avoid using the word to dignify one-off set-up jokes like 'Impasse'.

It's almost impossible to apply standard critical apparatus to a piece like this, because it has no pretensions beyond creating and then resolving a dilemma. At the time it helped me build my confidence, because by doing it I had proved to myself that I could write short fiction that would find publication, but the truth is that this kind of writing is always going to lead into a blind alley. At 650 words *Impasse* is probably just the right length.

Nicholson's Repentances

(OCTOBER 1965)

James Henry Nicholson was born on a Sunday. He was brought to life in a northern industrial town; in the shadow of a fog-blackened church, to the music of the monotone tolling of the bell and the damp touch of the insipid drizzling rain. His early life was like the town he lived in: drab and dull, coloured only by the poor respectability of his parents and neighbourhood. He attended church regularly, and became a leading member of' the Sunday School. One of his earliest memories was of church; standing near the front trying to sing a hymn while a woman in a flowered hat in the pew behind him sang loudly and prominently. He learned to hate this woman; her unmistakable soprano spoiled every hymn. As he grew older, he discovered this woman was the wife of the publican, a noted flirt and drunkard, and a rumoured adulteress.

This discovery was a turning point in the life of young Nicholson. In a way, this woman had been a symbol of' religion for him. Although he had hated her for the way she spoiled his songs, he'd held a grudging respect for her devoutness. At the age of eleven he found out what the words 'hypocrisy' and 'sanctimony' meant, and applied them immediately to the woman. As soon as he was able to break away from the restraint of his parents' influence, Nicholson stopped going to church. He formed a gang with some of his school friends, and on Sundays they'd plot elaborate conspiracies to murder the minister, blow up the church or steal the treasures inside it. They never came to anything, because Nicholson's friends did not have the same convictions to amplify their courage. As he grew into his teens, Nicholson deserted his gang, and began to study the theories of religion.

His education was a good one. He had never been unintelligent, and often showed brilliant promise in his school. He graduated into the local grammar school and, although he was unpopular, his studies flourished. He despised the morning services because of their total lack of meaning, and abhorred the Religious Instruction lessons because of their narrow approach. He borrowed and read every book in the school library on the subject of religion, and slowly began to form his own opinions on the subject.

When he was seventeen, he discovered what the word 'atheist' meant.

He left school, and pursued his studies no further. He obtained an insignificant job in the accounts department of a local factory. It was sufficiently remunerative to provide a modest income, and sufficiently undemanding to allow him to follow his spare time pursuits to the full. During the weekends he'd listen to the Salvation Army in the Town Hall square; he'd watch the devout coming out of church; and he'd listen to the hymns as he walked past churches, occasionally catching a distinctive phrase in a prominently loud soprano. Usually, he'd sneer to himself.

To him, God was nonexistent. He'd read the Bible when he'd been at school, and dismissed the Old Testament as myth elaborated by time; the New Testament as a historically valid document warped by imagination. Christ was a possible historical figure, but nothing more. Organized religion, he told himself, was an invention of Man, a necessary valve for expression. The people he hated most of all were churchgoers. To James Henry Nicholson, these were people who set values against belief, thinking that their neighbours would hold them in higher esteem for their devoutness. And to Nicholson, these people were worthy of one thing only: contempt.

His interests expanded as he grew older. He joined the British Nazi party, and spread his hatred to the minority religions and creeds. He affiliated himself to the Ku Klux Klan, and joined their mission against the coloured peoples of the world. His reputation grew in the newspapers over the years, and his name crept into the language of the world as another word with the same semantic connotations as Shelton, Rockwell and Hitler.

He died at an early age. It happened at a meeting in the dockland area of London when he'd been attempting to preach his own gospel, and the inevitable fighting had broken out. At one stage he was being ushered into a police van for his own protection, when a gun had exploded from nowhere. Two days later, in the cool white sanity of a hospital bed, surrounded by nurses, doctors and his parents, he passed restlessly from this life. Outside, the world breathed relief, thankful that his stay in this world had been so comparatively short. Only his parents mourned his passing.

But for Nicholson, the final reckoning was yet to come.

From the time of the shooting, his impressions had been rather confused. He was aware of pain, bright lights, and a lot of noise. Later, in the hospital bed, he had only the pain to contend with, and this was eased from time to time by injections. Somehow, there was always movement, and this distracted him. Then, the movement stopped, his pain vanished, and he slept.

He awoke, and found himself out in the open. The sky was a featureless grey, there was no wind, and no sun. He was standing at the foot of a broad stairway, which led up into a dimly visible perspective. At the top, Nicholson could just make out the outlines of a house.

There seemed nothing else to do, so he climbed the stairway. It was a steep climb, yet he felt no symptoms of tiredness. His body was active and whole, a machine with no bearings to wear out. After a long climb, he reached the house, and at the invitation of an anonymous sign, went straight inside.

There was a large spacious hall, decorated with many fine paintings and chandeliers. At the far side, there was a desk and a tired-looking clerk behind it.

When Nicholson reached the desk, the clerk looked up without interest.

'Name?'

'James Henry Nicholson.'

The clerk's manner changed immediately, a lustre of interest seemed to invigorate his eyes. 'Oh yes. We've been expecting you for a couple of days now.'

He reached across the desk, and depressed a switch on a speaker.

A voice said, 'Yes?'

'Nicholson's here, sir. I thought you might like to deal with him personally.'

'Yes indeed. I'll be up right away.'

The clerk released the switch, and stood up. 'We won't keep you a moment,' he said. He went over to a filing cabinet, and sorted through several cards. He selected one, sealed it in an envelope and handed it to Nicholson.

Just then, a door opened and a man came in. He was very tall, and carried a certain dignity in his manner.

He stood by the door, and held out his arm. 'Come this way, would you, Mr Nicholson,' he said politely.

Nicholson walked over to the door, and went through. He found himself in a small hall, at the junction of two stairways. One led up, losing itself in height, another led down into darkness.

The tall man laughed, in the jocular manner of the practised business executive. 'Well, Mr Nicholson,' he said. 'We know which staircase we're using, don't we?'

Nicholson nodded glumly, resigned to the worst. He led the way to the staircase, and began a slow descent. In the air, he fancied he could already smell the first hints of brimstone.

The stair wound down for what seemed like miles, then abruptly stopped by a stout wooden door. In front of it Nicholson stopped and turned. The tall man was behind him.

'I have to leave you here,' he said. 'This is the Gate of Hades. When you are ready, you go through, to smoulder for eternity.'

Nicholson swallowed. 'I'm ready now,' he said.

'Very well then,' the tall man said. 'I have to read you this.' He unrolled a piece of much used parchment, and cleared his throat. '"In the name of the Lord of Darkness whom I serve, by all the

Powers of Evil which I command, under the sign of the Holy Pentacle which rules me, and by all the Weapons of Damnation which I employ, I hereby consign you, James Henry Nicholson, to languish for Eternity in the bowels of Hell".'

The tall man re-rolled his parchment, nodded to Nicholson, and went back up the stairs.

Nicholson stood there for a short time, listening to the man's footsteps disappearing into the distance. When all was quiet, he caught hold of the door handle, and wrapped his hand around it. He looked around one more time, took a deep breath, and turned the handle.

He emerged into sunlight. As the door clanged back with a thudding note of finality, Nicholson took his first long look at Hell. He was standing on a wide grassy plain. The sky was blue, and dotted with white cumulus clouds. In the far distance, almost on the horizon, he could see a golden castle, tall pinnacles and silver spires. He took a few tentative steps forward.

A tambourine rattled, chord was struck. Around him, in roaring full-throated voice, the Choir of Angels launched into their first hymn, their high soprano voices in beautiful unison:

After the darkness, lo! the light
Shall all the past repair:
The perfect bliss, the spotless sight,
It is not here, but there.

Nicholson's Repentances - notes

Then:

John Wyndham's novel *The Chrysalids* makes several references to a culture-defining book called 'Nicholson's *Repentances.*' Although it is never described in detail, the reader gains the impression that *Repentances* is a grim religious tract, full of warnings about the evils of human mutation. (The theme of

Wyndham's novel.) I found the title and the author's name memorable, and used them for the title of this story.

The story is not autobiographical in any sense, even superficially, but it does reflect the feelings of an angry atheism that had grown in me through my teenage years. (This has mellowed subsequently to a more general doubting agnosticism.) With hindsight, I am surprised by how much I seem to have cared at the time, but I do think it was put on a bit for the sake of the story.

With all this hindsight possible after four decades, I realize that the story is structured rather like a joke: the set-up, the development, the twist ending. There is nothing particularly wrong in that, but that sort of simple structure is a limitation on what you can do with fiction.

There is no particular relevance to the words of the hymn quoted at the end. I was seeking something suitably pious, and found the words in an old hymnal. I wanted to avoid the familiar hymns.

This is (for me) a rare venture into fantasy. I don't recall offering it to any editors at the time, although there may be someone out there who remembers it.

Now:

The sentence structure is better again, although the semicolon in the second sentence is used incorrectly.

The use of vocabulary is surer than before, but the prose is plain.

The didactic style works better than the earlier attempts at lyricism, pastoralism, etc.

The staircase leading out of purgatory is over-familiar. Maybe I had seen the film *A Matter of Life and Death* recently?

Nicholson's wickedness does seem a bit strained. His joining of the British Nazi Party and the Ku Klux Klan is a sudden and extreme step, one for which the reader is not prepared in advance. Nicholson seems more of a disagreeable loony than an evil swine.

The implied meaning of the ending (hell is a personal matter) is not absolutely clear. Why is a heavenly host singing hymns such a terrible prospect for one such as Nicholson, about to suffer for all eternity?

I was 22 years old when I wrote *Nicholson's Repentances*, and after a short lifetime of reading books, casting columns of figures and generally lounging around I was not exactly equipped to write didactic fiction of this sort with any conviction. That is my main thought now, as I look at the story. There had been no climactic events that affected me in 1965, so there's nothing that I can reasonably think might have kicked this story off. However, I do know that it was the year when my reading tastes began to change again. I had discovered George Orwell's essays and articles, and developed a passion for them that continues to the present day. I had also started reading Graham Greene's novels, which I liked then much more than I do now. I read some Hemingway, Fitzgerald and a Canadian writer called Morley Callaghan (not unconnected with those two), whom no one apart from me seems to remember.

Perhaps from the unorganized mix of these writers came a new way of writing that I felt was worth a try.

The idea of an 'unorganized mix' is important to a writer. Until the period of 'Nicholson's Repentances', most of my reading while planning to become a writer had been science fiction. It was natural that I would gravitate to the form. But even then I was concerned that this gave a narrow view and helped restrict ambition.

I have always argued that the idiomatic nature of science fiction is its weakest attribute. The genre started as an imitative form in American 'pulp' magazines, where commercial writers vied with each other for publication space by imitating what had gone before.

It grew away from that through the activities of certain editors and writers, who brought more individual work to the fore, but it remains that there is much orthodoxy in SF: what it is deemed a writer might or might not write, that which is OK, that which is not. I was already feeling that pressure, and wanted to be free of it. It ingrained in me a lifetime habit of seeking the unorthodox, of going my own way. That much of my work falls into the loose category of the fantastic (or as SF itself, as it was defined in time more liberal than now) reflects mainly an interest in the fantastic as a source of interesting ideas and metaphors, rather than a wish to work inside that genre or any other.

It took years to throw off what I saw as genre preconceptions, because to be honest I shared them too in those early days. 'Nicholson's Repentances' seems to me now to represent the first moment when the restlessness began.

Combined Operation

(NOVEMBER 1965)

I was dozing between watches when the alarm blew: a raucous hounding of noise, reverberating around the narrow corridors. A ripple of excitement ran through the men, and as our armament was distributed our nerves exploded in a burst of obscenities.

We were silenced by the P.A. system. Preliminary identification pips sounded, then the flat and unemotional voice of our Colonel came over. He spoke quickly and simply, stressing the importance of our sortie, and the dangers we would face. Over his voice we could hear the mechanical straining of the troop-carrier as its motors were warmed and it roused its great bulk into action. This feeling of automated invincibility did more to sustain our morale than a dozen of the Colonel's speeches would have done. His voice died away, ending on a strained note of optimism.

Uncomfortably, we waited for the call to action, feeling the troop-carrier start to probe forward overhead. Our quarters were carried behind, storing us like seeds in a pod, waiting for the moment when our invasion could begin. The excitement was beginning to mount, seeming to climb in coils of nervous energy. Nobody said anything, we crouched there silently, listening for the signal. Time and again I checked my weapons. Deep down in my inside I could sense a tangible dread. It'll be *me* this time, I felt.

A yellow light started blinking: the troop-carrier had successfully entered the enemy country. Not long now. Around us we could feel the first concussions as the enemy's troops started to fight back. I resisted a sudden urge to jump up and rush to the carrier, blazing away with all the weapons I had. Not yet, not yet; wait for the signal. The concussions grew worse, and I wondered momentarily whether the operation could be stopped by the destruction of the troop-carrier. All my training came back to me, summed up in two basic concepts: trust your weapons, and obey your orders. The troop-carrier's fate was no concern of mine, if it was destroyed then it was too bad. Until then, wait for orders.

There was a louder and more prolonged concussion. In the same instant the P.A. crashed into life. *Action. Action. Action. Action.* Mindlessly I jumped to my feet, and ran down the corridors, metal boots ringing soundlessly. All around me, behind and in front, my comrades in arms ran too. With only one thought in mind, we ran as an organized military advance. As we got nearer to the carrier, our pace got faster and the corridor widened into the full area of the carrier's deck. Everywhere, silent explosions of incredible force rocked us and threatened our existence. In the same instance this was hell and heaven for me: the terrible fear of death, and the bliss of doing the job for which I had been trained.

Almost before I realized it, I had passed through the danger zone, and found myself lying on the enemy shore. Behind me, I could see the dark shape of the troop-carrier, still shaking under the impact of the enemy's weapons. The ground beneath me was still and quiet. I could see my comrades all about me, crouching low, as if recovering from the pounding we had all endured. Then, as if at an unspoken signal, we started creeping forwards into the unknown regions of the enemy land. To the rear, I heard the troop-carrier begin a relieved withdrawal, safe for another operation.

The advance took many hours. It was a slow wearying process, forever climbing a remorseless gradient, encountering all manner of obstacles. Almost from the time we left the shore, I felt as if I were on my own. Communications were nonexistent, and although I saw one or two of my comrades as we crept forward, no words were spoken. This was a personal war: each one of us seeking to fight the enemy for himself.

On and on I crawled. The further I went, the less I saw of my comrades. It felt as if the theatre of war had been allotted in sectors, one for each of us. Now completely alone, I crept onwards, getting steadily more and more tired. I had no rations with me, and I knew that unless I rejoined the main group soon, I was finished.

My fight became dual-purpose: not only to seek the enemy, but to stay alive too. As each minute dragged by, I could feel the chance slip away of either coming off. Weary, hungry, dirty and wet, I floundered on up the gradient.

And then I found the enemy.

I came on to it suddenly. It seemed to be resting in a small gully: a sphere of light several times larger than myself. It didn't see my approach; no movement showed over its whole repulsive body.

Race memories stirred in my mind. Here was the thing around the destruction of which I had built my whole life. Here, in front of me, was the eternal enemy of my people. And it was into my lap, my filthy, weary lap, that its destruction had fallen. Soundlessly, I crawled onwards, until its bulk loomed over me. I checked my weapons again, and found them all in order. I set the fuse on my grenade, cocked the firing lever, and braced myself.

Using all my remaining strength I jumped on to the loathsome side of its very body. The touch of its flesh sickened me. I could feel its nervous system stir sluggishly, awakening it to the realization that at last its existence had reached an end. Eternal, immortal combat. Locked forever in a battle neither of us could win. Great waves of nausea were rising in me and I fought them down. Impulsively I reached for the firing lever and, offering a quick prayer to my race, I pulled it.

My body vanished in a sheet of flame, fusing into the side of the being I had now destroyed. In my dying reaction, one last glimmer of realisation came to me:

At last – Conception.

Combined Operation - notes

Then:

Every beginning writer of SF, I fervently believe and hope, has the capacity to write a story such as 'Combined Operation.' I also hope and believe that it should only be written once. We should know better, but rarely do.

The notion of macro- or microscopy is almost irresistible. Those simplified drawings of atoms (nuclei with electrons orbiting about them) look just like tiny solar systems, with little suns and microscopic planets. An idea for a story! The two people from the Galactic Ordnance Division (G.O.D.) who land on an uninhabited planet and call themselves 8-M and E-V. An idea for a story! The deadly aliens who arrive on Earth and try to kill everyone, but discover too late they are the same size, and just as threatening to humans, as greenfly. An idea for a story! And, er, the soldier invading enemy territory who turns out to be a spermatazoon.

Although I was untutored as a writer, by the end of 1965 I should have known my SF clichés better. The only editor I sent this to was Michael Moorcock, at *New Worlds*. He rejected it at the speed of light, a favour for which I still silently thank him.

Now:

At least 'Combined Operation' is short.

Woody Allen filmed this, but I bet you didn't get paid for it. He made it funny, as it should have been all along, and put a pair of spectacles on his spermatozoon.

Don't do it again. (I didn't.)

I can't add more to the reasoning behind the writing of the story, except to put it in place in this book, a frank admission of having written a real turkey. If there is a moral it is that we should expect of a science fiction story more or less what we expect from any other fiction.

Some people think that SF has only ideas or notions, novelties or gimmicks, with which to play around. A story like 'Combined Operation' would seem to confirm this, but most SF is superior to this kind of thing.

The 'rules' for science fiction are much as the same as for all stories. It should have believable characters involved in a realistic situation, with genuine feelings, experiences and reactions. The fact that 'Combined Operation' has none of these is the real reason it's a poor story – that its central idea is corny only makes it worse. Its plot is again constructed like that of a joke, so that everything in the story is there as a build-up to the final revelation. If you are taken by surprise by the ending, or if you find it amusing, then the story has worked. My guess is that neither of these occurred, and so for most people the story won't have 'worked', even within its limited remit.

Let's move on. The rest of the stories are better.

The Ostrich Seed

(NOVEMBER 1965)

Housman awoke, feeling more foul than usual. The alarm he'd jury-rigged with pieces salvaged from the wrecked 'copter was buzzing incessantly, and the yellow signal over the tape unit was shining brightly. He climbed uncomfortably from his bunk, and disconnected the alarm; the tape-message could wait a little longer.

When the noise had stopped, Housman leaned against the control console, letting his head hang. He took a few deep breaths cautiously, trying to dispel the ache in his head. He mixed a powdery liquid from the medicine cabinet, and swilled it down.

As he waited for it to take effect, he looked around at the shambles in the dome. The happy-box had been wrenched away from the wall, its wiring littering the floor. As always, its red pilot light was glowing; a miracle considering the number of times he'd tried to adjust its controls. The desk was a mountain of books and papers, the bunk was a heap of loosely piled bedclothes, and the floor was strewn with cigarette ends and bottles. It would have looked, had an outside observer been able to see it, as if a party had been held in the dome for several days. In fact, it was the detritus of Housman's lone existence over the last year.

The only corner of the dome where there was anything like order was the area around the tape unit. As he looked at this again, he saw the yellow signal was still on. With an inexplicable sense of foreboding, he walked over to read the message. He flipped the switch, and the yellow light blinked out. There was a short silence, then the message was read over in clipped mechanical tones:

Central Control to Operative 17, Housman. Routine inspection of equipment and quota to be conducted 1400.23. Message ends.

Housman swore softly. He had known this was coming, yet he was almost totally unprepared for it. The only thing that he'd been able to keep looking as if it were respectable was the quota book, and that had been fabricated in one burst of energy several months before. The equipment was a different matter.

His mouth still felt hot and dry, though his head was beginning to feel more normal. He brewed some coffee on the autosupply, and dressed as he waited for it to come to the boil.
His clothes were clean and freshly pressed from the autosupply: in his year of increasing squalor, he'd retained a fastidious need to dress comfortably.

He sipped his coffee, and re-ran the message on the tape-unit. 1400.23 was yesterday. Typical of Central! What the message really meant, Housman guessed, was that they'd send an inspector as soon as they could; in the meantime, keep the house tidy. Looking around again at the dome, he wondered whether the implicit irony had been intended. Still, if the inspector was coming, it would be as well to give the machinery a quick check over. Momentarily, he remembered the alarm, and wondered what had broken down this time. He'd soon find out. He finished off his coffee, found his sun hat, and went out into the open air.

The sun had climbed fairly high and the glare from the desert hurt his eyes. He lowered his hat-brim a fraction and looked around to find where he'd left the half-track. It was parked about a hundred yards off, in the shadow of a large dune. As he walked across to it, Housman could feel the first pricking of perspiration in his armpits. The wind had been up again during the night, and there was a drift of the brown sand against the tracks, sifting in between the runner wheels.

He climbed up the hot metal of the ladder and into the cabin. The key was where he'd left it the afternoon before and he switched on. With a caution that was rare for him, he did a quick check on his dials: fuel, oil, battery and water. Everything seemed in order, and he pressed the starter. The huge engine turned and groaned, but didn't fire. He tried again, then again.

Damn! The sand must have blown in again.

He rummaged in the locker and found a flask. He took a small swig, reminding himself of the early hour, and climbed down again. He cleared the engine as well as he could, removing much of the superficial grit, and pushed away most of the drifted sand from the tracks.

He wiped his hands on a dirty rag he found in the back of the hot cabin, and pushed the starter again. This time the engine faltered into life on the fourth try. Gratefully, he let it have its head for a while, then eased in the gears and headed the half-track round in the direction of the Mining Multiple.

He opened the forward screen wide, and let the wind blow on his body. He still had no idea what had happened out at the Multiple, but whatever it was, it was unlikely to be anything he couldn't fix. The machinery was made as simple to maintain as possible, and provided the maintenance schedules were followed, nothing serious could go wrong. Although Housman's servicing was a long way in arrear, nothing had broken down to date that he hadn't been able to repair. Life suddenly became good for him, and he hummed quietly to himself. His hangover had now completely dispelled and, as he drove along, he took occasional nips at the flask. He caught a glimpse of his long, bearded face in the polished alloy of the fascia, and realized that he had lost a lot of weight since he'd been here. As far as he knew, he was alone on this planet; or if he wasn't, and there were other mining supervisors around, then for all the contact he had with them, he might as well be. Pity about the quota being behind, and the inspector coming. He was satisfied he could cover his trail with the falsified quota book, but the machinery was a problem. There was a good chance, though, that if the machinery looked as if it were working all right, then the inspector wouldn't look too closely at it. With any luck, Housman told himself, he'd probably be here and gone in a few days' time.

The half-track lurched on into the desert, its driver singing to himself at the controls.

When he reached the Mining Multiple, Housman found the reason for the alarm. Things were bad; worse than he could ever have imagined them to be.

The Multiple worked automatically and apart from frequent servicing needed no attention from its human supervisor. Basically, it was in two parts: the mining scoop itself, and the vast storehouse for the processed ores. The scoop was driven on huge banks of caterpillar tracks, which drove it across the desert like a mechanical mole. It swallowed the sand; analysed it, separated and rejected the unusable mineral sand, processed the ore into chunks of raw metal, and conveyed it back to the storehouse – all in one continuous operation. The Store contained massive bunkers to contain the processed ores, and a large computer which was used to plot the best lodes of the ochre-brown ore and guide the scoop on to them. The two units were connected by a large-diameter flexible pipe which served the dual purpose of being both a conveyor-belt for the processed ore, and an elaborate tow-rope for trailing the Store behind the mining scoop.

It was this pipeline which had broken.

The Store sat silently in the desert, a megatherian mound of metal stranded like some discarded toy. There was no sign of the scoop; with its built-in nuclear reactor, it had sufficient power to drive it many times around the girth of this planet.

Housman switched off the engine, and sat looking at the Store. His elation had suddenly vanished, he felt helpless.

He climbed out of the cabin, and walked around to the front of the unit. The silence was uncanny, exaggerated by the towering height of the Store. The pipeline had snapped very near the scoop: the lubrication of the flexible pipe was one of those tasks he'd neglected to do, thinking it was unnecessary labour. The broken end of the pipe was ragged; about a hundred yards from it he could see a processed ingot of ore, dropped like anal discharge from the foreshortened stub of the trailing pipeline.

He climbed up to the service bay in the Store, and looked out across the desert. Towards the horizon, a range of purple cliffs reared into the sky in atomillo perspective. A line of abandoned ingots curved towards them, then doubled back wildly, running parallel for thousands of yards. Then the line twisted again, and disappeared. For a moment, Housman wondered at the apparent randomness of the line, then realised that the scoop was still doggedly following the last course computed for it.

That gave him an idea. He quickly coded a question and fed it into the computer. The reply came out almost at once, giving him a full extrapolation of the scoop's course, based on unadjusted readings. He computed the exact time the scoop had broken away, and the estimated speed at which it would now travel without the hindering weight of the trailed Store. Housman worked deftly, using old skills which he'd forgotten he had. There was still time, possibly, to give chase and switch off the scoop. Time, even, to get it back here and re-attach it to the Store before the inspector arrived.

The scoop's course was a series of erratic and random loops, forward and backwards across the valley, up and down its length. Working quickly, with the aid of a map and the computer, Housman soon plotted the scoop.

Unbelievingly, he straightened. His lucklessness was unbelievable, and equally undeniable. Assuming his calculations to be correct (and the use of the computer obviated any reasonable doubt) then the scoop would be passing in the immediate vicinity of the dome within the next three hours. In two hours and forty-eight minutes, to be precise. With his luck, it would probably demolish the dome completely.

At least he now knew where the scoop was, or would be!

He grabbed his sun hat from where he'd thrown it, climbed down from the service bay, and sprinted back to the half-track.

When he got back to the dome, there was a slim planet ship parked beside it.

He climbed out on to the half-track's engine compartment, and waved his hat at the man who was standing by the dome, peering in at the chaos. The man walked across to him.

'Housman? I'm Rushton, they've sent me from Central.'

'Yes, I know. I received the message this morning.' He looked carefully at the newcomer. He was a short man, fairly stout yet not uncomfortably fat. He had long hair, flopping across his face. Sweat was already darkening his shirt.

'I can't stay too long today,' he said. 'I've got another operative to visit this week. If you don't mind I'll get straight down to business.'

Housman looked steadily at the man, trying not to betray his agitation. 'Suits me,' he said. 'Would you care for a drink?' He looked around at the horizon. Was that just his imagination, or could he really hear already the faint distant racket of the scoop homing in on his dome?

The inspector followed his glance. 'No. I don't drink, thanks.' He narrowed his eyes against the glare. 'Hot weather you have here. Plays hell with the machinery I should think.'

Housman nodded. 'That's right,' he said. 'Shall I get you the quota book? I brought it up to date this morning after I was notified you were coming.'

He jumped down from the hot metal and walked to the dome, congratulating himself on his foresight. Rushton followed him into the dome, watching him shrewdly. The quota book was on the desk, and after a quick search, Housman found it. He gave it to the inspector and turned away, wishing he'd hurry.

Rushton scanned the book cursorily, flipping sheets casually. 'These seem to be all right,' he remarked at length. 'I'll have to inspect the machinery as well, though.'

Housman stared out across the brown desert, not taking any notice of the inspector. He was wondering how he could get the man away in time to be able to intercept the scoop before it reached the dome. The more he thought about it, the less his chances figured. He wondered how much effect the incidence of dunes and boulders would have on the course of' the scoop. Not much, he calculated.

His attention was broken by the inspector pulling at his arm.

'Sorry,' he said. 'I was thinking of something else.'

'I was asking about the machinery. It is all right, isn't it?'

Housman felt an ominous sensation in his stomach. He should have known that he never stood a chance of getting away with it. He turned away again, and fidgeted with the controls of the happy-box. 'No,' he said finally. ''The machinery isn't working entirely as it should. I had to falsify the quota book. The Multiple hasn't worked properly for months.'

He looked back at the inspector, who had the faintest hint of a smile hovering around his eyes. 'What happened?' Rushton said.

Housman thought quickly. 'I had an accident,' he said, on a sudden idea. 'The 'copter went down a crevasse, taking the servicing gear with it.'

The inspector's smile broadened fractionally. (The bastard! Housman thought. He's enjoying this.) 'Just as well then,' Rushton said, 'that I've got spare gear in the ship.'

For the second time that day, the half-track crawled across the dull brown wastes of the desert. Even in the short time between trips, the trail had been covered slightly by the ever-drifting grit. Behind the half-track a cloud of dust hung in the air, like the spray from a fast launch.

Housman was thinking hard. Rushton's reaction to his story had been calm and slightly amused. He even seemed to understand about the machinery being broken. He'd told the inspector, almost in a mood of confession, and the man had been irritatingly unruffled. Even the lame excuse about the 'copter, half true as it was, had been accepted. He wondered what Rushton's reaction would be when he found out about the broken pipeline. Not long now, and he'd find out. He looked at his wristwatch. In about twenty minutes from now the scoop would be at the dome. It was too late to do anything about it; all he could do was to hope it would miss. Dismissing the idea, he turned to Rushton who was sitting with his legs braced against the lurching of the vehicle.

'How's the war going these days?' he shouted over the roar of the engine and the rattle of the servicing gear in the locker behind them.

The inspector looked thoughtful. 'Not well.'

'No? Are we losing ground then?'

'At the moment we seem to be losing everything: planets, ships, and lives. Tau Ceti sector fell a few days ago. In terms of lost life, the greatest human tragedy in history.'

'What's gone wrong?' Housman asked. 'I thought our weapons were superior, and we had more of them.'

Rushton glanced at him. 'We're short of raw materials, man. We've got the men and machinery to build the ships, and we've got the arsenals waiting to turn out the weapons. We've got the knowledge and resource to design bigger and better of both. But we've got no metals or fuels.'

'I see.' Housman looked straight forward, a terrible complex of guilt hitting him hard. Down here on a backwater planet, alone and away from the heart of things, a man could forget the war. He could pretend it didn't exist, and wrap himself in a protecting field of diversion. He realized now that in the months in which he'd been here, the need to produce metal had lost its purpose, and had been replaced by a passive routine.

And as he'd sat there in his comfortable dome, addicting himself to the happy-box, a war was being lost.

'There's something else as well,' Rushton went on. 'Somewhere along the line the human race has lost its guts. That knowledge and resource I mentioned doesn't exist any more. "To hell with the war," that's what they say these days. Look at you with your pitiful quota juggling. Look at all of us, letting the ground rot beneath our feet. I'm as bad as the rest of them: I wouldn't have come even here, if I hadn't lost my family in Tau Ceti.'

'I'm sorry,' Housman muttered weakly, not audible in the din of the engine. He drove on for a few minutes, subconsciously connecting the erosion of human guts with the insidious drifting of the sand on this wretched planet.

The half-track breasted a large, high dune, and he stopped it at the crest. About half a mile away the Store was plainly visible, standing alone and dignified. He could see the curling trail of excreted ingots, twisting away out of sight.

'I don't think we need go any further,' he said. 'The Store is half full, and is never likely to be filled again. The scoop broke away yesterday.'

Rushton looked down on the dismal scene for a moment or two. The sand was already starting to drift against the side of the vast machine. Another month, and it would probably be completely covered.

'Things could be worse, I suppose,' he said finally. 'You've collected some ore, which is more than some operatives I've visited.'

'Seen enough?' Housman asked. 'The sight depresses me now.' He looked again at his watch, and winced slightly. While they'd been talking the moment had come and gone.

He pushed the starter and the diesel engine roared into life again. He turned the wheel, and headed the half-track back in the direction of the dome. As it ploughed across the desert, neither he nor the inspector said anything. As far as Housman was concerned, the episode was finished. The war was as good as lost and remaining on the planet would now serve no useful purpose. His one thought was to leave. Rushton had offered no explanation for the inertia, but Housman knew somehow that he was right. Why fight superior enemies? Why fight the war, this planet or any one of the forces constantly opposing life? The easy way out was a strong temptation in certain circumstances.

They came up to the dome, climbing the slow rise that lay before it. Even from a distance, Housman could see the wreckage. The scoop had justified his worst fears, and ploughed straight into the dome. It had come to rest halfway into the building, its tracks straining still against the piled wreckage. Out of the truncated tube attached to the rear of the scoop's body, Housman could see the beginnings of another ingot. He had a fleeting vision of a wealth of processed ore, forever lost in the bistre sand, lying in a bizarre and random trail across the desert.

In the metal maw of the machinery lay the remains of the planet ship.

Suddenly Housman laughed. He stopped the half-track, jumped down on to the sand, and leaned against the cowling, laughing until his eyes watered profusely. Rushton stood with him, roaring too. Still laughing, they staggered across to the landed scoop, half blinded by the thrown cloud of brown dust. Housman jumped on to the vibrating body of the machine, lifted a small hood, and pulled a lever. Immediately, the violent grinding of the nuclear gears dropped away, and an insipid silence fell.

Still choking slightly with laughter, Housman looked at Rushton. The inspector was fishing through the crumpled remains of his ship, a strange kind of smile giving his face a dazed expression.

Housman jumped down, and stepped past him into the dome. Through the swirling dust, now beginning to settle, Housman looked at the desolation. Most of the dome had been wrecked: the tape unit had disappeared under the crush of one of the caterpillar treads; so too had the auto-supply, which provided all the food. The happy-box was miraculously undamaged, its pilot light glowing defiantly. His desk had been knocked on to its side, and his papers and books lay in a dusty pile in the shattered remains of the bottles and glasses.

Rushton came in behind him. 'The ship is a write-off. To hell with it. Even if those prats in Central were interested enough to listen to us, they'd never believe us. They've probably forgotten I'm here, anyway.'

Housman, wondering how he'd known Rushton was going to say that, said, 'The happy-box is working.'

Rushton started laughing again. 'So what have we got to worry about?' he asked logically.

Picking a bent paperbacked book from the debris beneath the desk, Housman walked out into the sun. He sat down on the sand,

and leaned against the side of the mining scoop. Behind him in the dome, he heard the happy-box hum as Rushton warmed up the circuits.

The Ostrich Seed - notes

Then:
'The Ostrich Seed' was an attempt to write a real SF story, one with a legitimate idea, setting, and so on. Although I did not plan it consciously that way, certain of the attitudes found in Robert Sheckley's marvellous short stories can be found here. But Sheckley would have made the idea both more fiendish and funny: for instance, the problem with the scoop would have been more ingenious than just having it break away, and he would have made the inspector, Rushton, into something more than the dullard I came up with.

In the clause 'a range of purple cliffs reared into the sky in atomillo perspective,' I coined a new word. Frequent checks in the Supplement to the *Oxford English Dictionary* have not found it to be in general usage, so I assume after forty years it's not going to catch on.

I seem to remember this story was offered to the editors of both *New Worlds* and *Impulse*, without success.

Now:
The use of narrative English shows a real improvement on the past. Most of the sentences are well formed. The pace is good, if a bit thin in detail. The narrative ability is OK.

But the use of verbs is lacklustre. The constant use of 'got', for instance. In one short piece of dialogue we have: 'got the men and machinery', 'got the arsenals', 'got the knowledge', 'got no metals'. (There are several other occurrences elsewhere.)

Where more ornate verbs are used, they seem a bit dodgy:

'the use of the computer obviated any reasonable doubt' ('removed' would have been better), and 'The scoop had justified his worst fears' (better written intransitively as: 'His worst fears were substantiated/justified/confirmed/vindicated by ...').

There's quite a good image of the Store stuck by itself in the desert, which George Lucas no doubt pinched for the first *Star Wars* film, but now I stumble over the word 'megatherian' and wonder what it means. Back in 1965 I remember believing that it was some kind of dinosaur, presumably large and probably slow-moving, and thus an appropriate metaphor to use for a big machine that was no longer working. Looking it up in a dictionary forty years after I should have done I belatedly discover that a megathere is a kind of giant sloth, long extinct, a native of North America. In a loose sense it was therefore a dinosaur, but I think using the word as an adjective was probably inappropriate in the context. At least a sloth moves slowly.

Repetitions: 'The Store *contained* massive bunkers to *contain* the processed ores', and '*Unbelievingly*, he straightened. His lucklessness was *unbelievable*.'

There's a fair amount of SF jargon in the story, which I see now as a sign of nervousness and inexperience. In 1965, inexperience was obviously the excuse for me, but with writers who have been publishing for some time this kind of shorthand is usually caused by laziness. We shouldn't have to use the shorthand of other writers.

Some of the jargon in 'The Ostrich Seed' is mild and self-explanatory. 'Central Control' is the sort of thing you used to come across in those black-and-white BBC-TV dramatizations of SF stories in the 1970s, Central Control usually being represented by a plywood cabinet with dials, lights and a loudspeaker grille. A 'happy-box' also speaks for itself, as does 'autosupply', but using 'ship' in the way it is used here is a misnomer that is both common in and typical of the most uninteresting kinds of SF.

The Ostrich Seed

At least 'The Ostrich Seed' is a proper story with a situation, a problem, a resolution and finally some kind of point. At some 3,500 words it doesn't outstay its welcome.

The Ersatz Wine

(MARCH 1966)

Hawkins ran steadily down the darkness of the straight cobbled street. It had rained earlier, and the stones were still slick with moisture. Now the sky was clear, and he could vaguely define some of his surroundings. He was in a quarter of the town he'd never visited before. Occasionally he heard deep-throated sirens in the near distance, and guessed he was in the vicinity of the docks. Once, as be ran under an iron railway bridge, a long goods train clanked overhead.

'Hurry up there,' shouted the Pilot. 'I've got three more fields to dust before the day's out.'

Hawkins crossed a brightly lit main road, spangled with neon shops and incandescent signs. Feeling as if he were crossing enemy lines in the flood of a searchlight, he dived for cover into a welcoming alleyway. Behind him, the traffic closed around the breach he had caused as he crossed.

'My theme for today', said the Preacher, 'is the meaning God holds for us in our everyday lives. Far too often, God is just an idea, not a presence. He holds perpetual court to all His subjects, yet only rarely does He take homage. It is our duty, as citizens in His universal kingdom, to be constantly ...'

A row of dustbins lined one of the walls, and Hawkins slid to a halt beside them. He ducked down, and leaned against the wall. His head lolled backwards, and he took deep breaths gratefully. A smell of oily food drifted out of a ventilation grille directly above his face.

'Backstage I'm lonely, Backstage I cry,' said the Pop Singer.

Hawkins listened carefully. There was no sound he could directly identify as his pursuers. About twenty yards from where he squatted, he could see the traffic crawling past the mouth of the alley. Occasionally a horn sounded or brakes grated. Music from a nearby pub drifted to him in patches. His breath was steadying now. Already he was feeling better for having rested.

'Ours is work of creation,' said the Architect. 'We mould in concrete and glass, and paint with woodwork and brass. We sculpt on the grand scale. Whole cities are shaped by our pencils.'

He stiffened suddenly. He heard voices being raised, and an animal snuffling at the pavement. He levered himself from the ground and backed away along the wall. A doorway presented itself to him, and he flattened his body inside it. Behind the door he could hear movement.

'All prices slashed by 10%. Double stamps on Tuesdays, and fifty extra on every economy-sized packet of Daz.'

A torch flashed at the mouth of the alley. Its tight brilliant beam flashed expertly around the alleyway, at one point missing Hawkins' head by a matter of inches. He pressed harder against the doorway, and felt it give slightly. On an impulse, he seized the handle and turned it.

'In a torrid sunset,' said the Author, 'the heroine dies. Her lover, a man of stature in the world of politics, has left her in the cause of his own career. Too late, her ex-fiancé, whom she'd left for the politician, realizes her plight. He finds her on the sand, her hair playing free in the flowing tide.'

The hallway was a bright splash of light, compared with the darkness of the alley. A slim, dark-haired girl was sitting on the bottom step of a flight of stairs. She looked up at him and smiled.

'I think it's the drum-sound that gets them,' said the Leader of the pop-group. ''It's hollow, you see ...'

Hawkins stared at the girl. As she stood up, he could see that she was holding a grey kitten in her left hand. She fondled it constantly with her other hand, its head rubbing upwards against the pressure. She put the kitten down, and held out her hand towards Hawkins.

The Beautician grinned shrewdly at the Interviewer. 'Yes,' she said. 'You could put it like that, I suppose. We achieve nothing more than a very *superficial* success.'

Hawkins listened at the door for a couple of moments. Hearing nothing, he straightened, as if in relief. He saw that the girl was smiling at him. Her hand was still held out towards him. Tentatively, he stretched out his own hand towards her. Together, they walked slowly up the stairs.

The Shop-Steward said, 'Our local executive has negotiated with the employers' representative. No agreement was reached, on any single count. We have just received an official directive from the regional office to the effect that, pending final negotiations, we down tools from Thursday next.'

Her room was small and dark. A fan-heater by the cupboard was turning quietly, filling the entire room with dry heat. Two pairs of stockings hung from a piece of string looped across the window. She switched on a low table lamp by the bed, and turned off the central light. Hawkins looked cautiously through the window, but could see very little. Her room overlooked the alley in which he'd been hiding. He could see no sign of his pursuers.

The Doctor signed the prescription wearily. 'I've given you a tonic, Mrs. Williams,' he said. 'It should make the world of difference.'

He looked back at the girl. She was unbuttoning her blouse. She smiled at him again, and held out her hand. He went to her, and took her in his arms. They kissed warily, then firmly. After a while, they sank on to the bed, and Hawkins groped gently for her breasts. She responded fiercely, kissing him with shaking strength as he pulled her blouse from her and released her brassière.

'It'll be ready tomorrow,' said the Garage Proprietor. 'I'll have to send away for some spare parts. We're right out of them at the moment.'

The rest of their clothes came away in hurried fumblings of fingers. Finally, they lay together on the top of the bed, their skins moulding together where they touched.

'The object of the exercise,' said the Subaltern, 'is to take this enemy stronghold ... here.' He placed a yellow-headed pin into a map of the Rhine country. 'The enemy will be troops from the American forces, and will be identified by red armbands. Smoke bombs and dummy mortars will be the armaments of the enemy ...'

She kissed his neck tenderly, as he stroked her soft white skin. Slowly, their caresses became more strident and bold. They rolled and stretched on the bed, their clothes kicked into a forgotten heap at the foot.

'Smoke Players Medium,' said the Advertising Hoarding. Behind the legend, a pair of hands was removing the cellophane from the pack with lascivious movement. A large mouth sucked extravagantly on the smoke.

Soon, they quietened. They lay together, still linked, and spoke voicelessly together. Their skin was damp from their exertions, and their hair mussed. She held him to her, almost possessively.

'Two fat ladies: eighty-eight,' said the Bingo-caller. 'Three and seven: thirty-seven. Key of the door: twenty-one. On its own: number six ...'

After a few minutes he pulled away from her and went to the sink. He washed thoroughly, rinsing his face and hands in the cold water. He dressed slowly, watching his reflection in the tall mirror on the door of the wardrobe. Behind him. the girl still lay on the bed.

'My work,' said the Artist, 'is a total expression of my soul. It relates in terms of colour and image the visual interpretation of consciousness.' His audience nodded and smiled. staring in serious awe at the canvas behind the Artist. It was daubed with shredded inner-tubes and random streaks of motor-oil.

As he shut the door behind him, Hawkins took one last look at the girl. She was lying facing towards him. Her eyes were shut, with a hint of tears about to roll on to her cheeks. Her legs still stretched across the bed, unmoved. He shut the door firmly, and walked cautiously down the stairs. At the bottom, a grey kitten mewed at him.

'... Surely goodness and mercy shall follow me all the days of my life: and I will dwell in the house of the Lord for ever ...'

Hawkins walked out into the alley. It was darker there now, the lights in the main road having dimmed. The traffic was lighter now, only the occasional vehicle speeding through. His body ached, and his mouth felt dry.

The French starlet in the mink coat smiled at the cameras. 'I hereby open this wonderful new flyover,'she read from her notes. Behind her, a thousand cars growled on the starting-line.

He wandered away from the alley, across the main road and into the maze of streets behind the docks. He walked for hours, steadily tiring. At last he could go no further.

None of his muscles reacted to his signals for motion, his sight was blurring, and his hearing was becoming weaker.

'What right have we to keep this man alive?' demanded the Surgeon. 'Transistors and batteries are bastardizing God's work!'

His pursuers found him in the morning. He was leaning against a pile of crates in the harbourmaster's yard. They took him back to the hospital, trying to think of some way of keeping his batteries charged.

'My life,' said the Actor, 'is a constant lie.'

The Ersatz Wine - notes

Then:

This was the first story I sold to *New Worlds*, which at the time felt like a real breakthrough. In 1966, *New Worlds* represented the cutting edge. It was where all the best young writers of the time wanted to appear. This is not the place to go over the history of *New Worlds*, except to say that after some twenty years as a traditional science fiction magazine, publishing planetary and futuristic stories, *New Worlds* had found a new editor in Michael Moorcock. He had taken over a couple of years before I wrote this story. Moorcock had strong ideas about modern fiction, and for a time at least used *New Worlds* as a platform for his views. He published many more younger and newer writers than before, while at the same time he encouraged established writers, notably Brian Aldiss and J. G. Ballard, to throw off any shackles from the past by which they might have been feeling held back.

Although almost anything was better than the derivative and tired material that had been published before, the problem with the new *New Worlds* was that it soon became a self-sustaining and self-referential school of trendy attitudes. Moorcock, a mercurial figure, had the knack of attracting followers and hangers-on, some of them terrible drags and boors. Because of his own liberal instincts Moorcock allowed some of the more witless ones too much say in the direction the magazine might take.

At the time I wrote this story I don't think I was aware of how far that was processing, but in a sense 'The Ersatz Wine' had become a part of the result. I see it now very much as a *New Worlds* 'type' of story, quite different from the work I had done before – no bad thing, of course – but also not at all indicative of what I was to write later on. (See the comments on the story 'Conjugation', following, where Moorcock has something to say which I found, in the end, extremely useful.)

It was not the first story of mine to be published in *New Worlds* – that fell to 'Conjugation'. I should have preferred 'The Ersatz Wine' to be published first, but for alleged reasons of lack of space that did not happen.

It turned up in *New Worlds* for March 1967 (No. 171), the main compensation being that the title and my name were featured on the front cover. As I shared this billing with the first (slightly shortened) appearance of Brian Aldiss's novel *Report on Probability A* and J. G. Ballard's famous short story 'The Assassination of John Fitzgerald Kennedy Considered as a Downhill Motor Race' I felt I was keeping wonderful company. With these long titles spreading out for line after line, it's surprising there was still room for me on the limited space of *New Worlds*' cover.

'The Ersatz Wine', as I say, was written as a self-conscious attempt to emulate some of the effects of the 'new wave' then current. Although I was never really much involved with the new wave (in it, but not of it, I always say), the times were undoubtedly exciting for a young writer. Being impressionable and eager to succeed, for a while it felt to me that that was the way to go. It is neither a good, bad nor typical example of the new wave kind of story.

I meant the story to be a sort of exposé of the brittle, artificial world of glittering surfaces that I detected all around me. Well, it sounded good to me at the time. Perhaps my artistic vision was a little blurred by the mistaken belief I then had, that 'ersatz' meant false or fake. Its true meaning of substitute or imitation isn't quite the same thing as I intended. Even with this in mind, I have felt ever since the story first appeared that the title would have been better without the definite article.

Although the story was published with reasonable prominence, *New Worlds* was by then in its dying days as a paperback magazine, and had only a small readership. I have never had the story reprinted and I don't recall anyone ever mentioning it to me. Hence its inclusion here.

> *Now:*
> The sentences are in general good. The style is straightforward and declarative, the viewpoint detached. This gives an impression of exactness, but also of distance from feelings. Perhaps this is suitable, bearing in mind what we learn about Hawkins at the end.
>
> Some of the writing misses the target, but only just. Some examples:
>
> 'He could vaguely define some of his surroundings.' – 'Make out' or 'discern' his surroundings would be better. And once a writer starts admitting things look a bit vague he runs the risk of letting his readers lose their own focus on the story.
>
> 'There was no sound he could directly identify as his pursuers.' – Either the sounds should be made plural, or his

pursuers should have a possessive apostrophe ... but 'He could not hear his pursuers' would probably be better for being simpler.

'A fan-heater by the cupboard was turning quietly, filling the entire room with dry heat.' – Lines like this always make me wonder where you can buy a fan-heater that will fill only part of a room with heat.

'Slowly, their caresses became more strident and bold.' – 'Bold' is OK, with the meaning of increasing intimacy, but 'strident' (which usually means sounds, not actions) would never be right.

'They lay together, still linked, and spoke voicelessly together.' – This opens up the unspoken question, briefly reproduced as: '   ?'

I feel now that the story is wilfully obscure, although you can more or less work out what was going on by the end. I once characterized the typical *New Worlds* story from this period as being about drugs and turds and guitars in Notting Hill. At least 'The Ersatz Wine' avoids all that over-familiar riff.

Conjugation

(May 1966)

Extract From The Diary of 1st-class Spaceman Stolanski.

New York and Kennedy, pleasant sight. Home, and six years' wandering. Wife? Jean and the kids ... three at the last count. More? Not Jean. Faithful as a dog, my Jean. Weather lousy. Goddam rain in September ... clouds visible from here. Still in orbit ... hell! So near to home.

Something wrong, though. What?

Part of An Address by Professor T. N. Williamson, PhD, to the Alfred Korzybski Institute.

Circumstances of existence, and theories of evolution. Semantics with emphasis on language and communication of idea. Required integration and cohesion impossible without full development of parsing and syntax. Comprehension, for instance, of an idea without the necessary background information not entirely feasible.

Minor Passage From the Ms. of An Unfinished Novel by Kenneth G. Robbs.

The city, in its black mantle of night, with its covert impressions of movement, with its traffic and its arteries of steel, and its hive-bound humans. Two, man and girl, in love. Conversation:

'Your eyes and your hair. Beauty.' This to Annette.

'Humour and understanding, Jack.'

The man with a laugh on his face. Kiss in a doorway, and caresses beneath clothing. Stronger feelings of love and understanding. Taxi to her flat, and hurried intercourse in the dark. More conversation:

Annette: 'My darling. So strong and smooth.'
Jack: 'All yours. Taken in love.'

REPORT FROM THE NEWS-PAGE OF THE *NEW YORK TIMES*.

18th September, 2048. Kennedy Port, N.Y. Return from space: *Outwarder II*. Crew well, and equipment in order. Captain, Commander D. H. ('Dannie') Ross, in press-conference at VIP lounge. Report: 'Swell trip.'

His wife, Miriam Avril Ross (29) and his two fine lads Mike (8) and Billy (6) the centre of attraction. Question to Mrs. Ross, about her husband's flight.

'Just happy. My Dannie back so soon.'

FRAGMENT OF TAPE-RECORDED CONVERSATION AT THE NINTH ANNUAL REUNION OF THE LITERATURE RESTORATION SOCIETY.

'The apostrophe more vital in contemporary thought.'

'How so?'

'Instanced example. *Finnegan's Wake* in early 20th Century renaissance. The apostrophe ambivalent. The Wake *of* Finnegan? Or ...'

'Your reasoning insecure.'

'No no, unfinished development of my idea.'

'Continuing? Apologies for interruption.'

'The Wake of Finnegan. Or ... Something else. What?'

ENTRY IN THE EMERGENCY-LOG OF FIRE-CHIEF WATSON, *KENNEDY PORT*.

9:19:48. 16:03 hrs.

Landing Area: TK. Co-ordinates 783/298.

Crew: Mitchison Cowley Atzatchek Pallini Kearley & Rico.

Scramble-code 19, buzzer in fire-dispersal building and klaxon on main building. Check with Central, explosion in *Outwarder II*. Selection: Tender F.

Arrival at point of explosion. Much smoke and debris. No immediate evidence of fire. Check.

Damaged space-module at approximately 15 deg. list. Utilization of buttressing equipment: prompt forestalling of any danger of collapse. (Commendation: Atzatchek.
Initiative and disregard for personal safety). Check.

Thorough inspection of space-module. Attached inventory of damaged equipment (per Cat. 109657) self-explanatory.

Return to fire-dispersal. Check.

TRANSCRIPTION (EXP.) OF VIDEOTAPED NETWORK PLAY EARLY ON THE EVENING OF 17TH SEPTEMBER.

End of sponsor's announcement. Fade.

Fade-in credits. ('MESCALINE PASSIONATE' Pt. III). Theme music.

Fade-out music and credits.

Scene: Hotel bedroom. Mescaline in bed, her back to the camera. Door (r.) and Francesca entrance. Bath-robe loose across her breasts.

MESCALINE

(appreciative glance at F.)

This heat ... intolerable.

FRANCESCA

Drink? Only cold thing here, water. Wonder-worker on whisky. (*Her hand at her robe. Slow movement of hand.*)

MESCALINE

(movement from bed to F.)

Frank.

BRIEF PRECIS OF THE REGULAR SCIENCE COLUMN IN THE LAST-KNOWN EDITION OF THE *TRIBUNE*.

19 September. Damage to drive-compartment of *Outwarder II.* Not an explosion, as first. Spontaneous, total *implosion* perhaps. Drive-compartment a total ruin. Smoke still very evident. Tests in laboratory, on nature of the smoke, results widely varied. Non-igneous, non-toxic, no solid state yet discovered. Dispersion

quotient nonexistent; even in high winds.

Tests on the passed water of the returned astronauts. Similar results. Blood tests on 1st Class Spaceman Stolanski, shortly prior to his sudden death, with same result. No evident unifying factor. Urine and blood with no state other than a liquid one? Smoke with no state other than gaseous? All totally inert?

UNUSED SCRIPT FOR AN ADDRESS BY THE PRESIDENT ON THE EVENING OF THE TWENTIETH. ORIGINAL CONTEXT NOW UNCERTAIN.

Our nation, historically sound, proven stable and wise, constant adversary of the warmonger, now at a new stage. Your government in the face of an adversary incomprehensible and intangible. The menace more terrible because so unimaginable. Your lives in continuance as before, yet under the shadow of something.

Only one question now. What?

The answer outside our comprehension. At present.

PART OF THE LAST NEWS-SHEET TO BE HANDED OUT IMMEDIATELY PRIOR TO THE DECLARATION OF MARTIAL LAW IN ALL CITIES OF A POPULATION EXCEEDING 60,000.

9:20:48. Commander 'Dannie' Ross, late of the *Outwarder*. Missing. Last sighting at Kennedy Port, in the vicinity of the wreck of his late ship. Search later: no trace of Ross. No possible means of exit from the field.

MESSAGE RECOVERED FROM THE WRECKAGE OF A BOEING STRATOSPHERIC, WASHED ASHORE ON LONG ISLAND REACH.

... flight otherwise routine. Most passengers and crew unconscious now. No reply from Kennedy. Baltimore: homing signal, but no other response. Landing impossible without base servos. Twenty minutes to ETA. Further attempt in ten minutes ...

FRAGMENT OF PAPER FOUND ON THE BODY OF FIRE-TENDER OPERATIVE ATZATCHEK.

My buddies, in panic. Like a rabble. That noise, my God. Like a turbo, only worse. Close, too. And that smoke. Movement like water, except faster.

Then I look, and *Outwarder* has gone. What the hell? The smoke's still here, though. Wish I knew what to do.

The smoke's thickening, and the noise is getting louder. Holy Maria, what a racket! Wish I knew what –

Conjugation - notes

Then:

Although published before 'The Ersatz Wine', in the December 1966 edition of *New Worlds* (No. 169), this was actually the second story I sold to the magazine.

Presumably because it followed a couple of months after I had sent him 'The Ersatz Wine', Michael Moorcock said when accepting 'Conjugation' that he was going to buy and print the story, but that he did not think it was necessarily the right direction for my writing to take.

At the time I thought this was a bit rich, coming from an editor who was privately and publicly urging his contributors to experiment with new ways of telling stories, but four decades down the line I can see his point. There was, there *is*, no future in this kind of writing.

It was actually remarkably easy to turn out stuff like 'Conjugation', while conventional prose was still full of difficulties. But as I think Mike Moorcock sensed, it wasn't what I was going to be able to keep up for much longer.

So, what was going on here? A clue to the embarrassing explanation of 'Conjugation' lies in the title. I was wondering aloud what the English language would be like, what you could do with it, if you suddenly removed all the verbs and the verb-forms. There are vague hints in the story that an external presence or force aboard a returning spaceship is responsible, Quatermass-like, for this, but in essence it is a short story where the writer is playing around with words.

I haven't been tempted to try anything like it since.

Now:

You're playing around with words.

The story is not short enough.

'Swell' is out-dated American slang. It was out-dated in 1966.

You're confused about the title of *Finnegans Wake*, and I suspect you brought it into the story as a cover, summoning Joyce as a kind of pre-emptive defence. Own up: you've never read *Finnegans Wake*.

I still don't understand the story, and I have read almost one whole page of *Finnegans Wake*.

Not long after 'Conjugation' was published I was contacted by another *New Worlds* contributor, who happened to live near me. He had read both of my stories, while I had also seen some of his in the magazine. In truth I had never been able to make head nor tail of them, so I was a bit nervous before the meeting, fearing he might be brainy and/or deep. In reality, he was a pleasant and unassuming guy, working in London in a full-time job, but with grand aspirations for his writing. I shared those aspirations with him, so we had an enjoyable evening in a pub together.

Towards the end of the evening we veered into the subject of 'stream of consciousness' writing, or Brion Gysin's 'cut-up' method, or general use of language in a concrete way. We found we were at odds.

He said he saw the deconstruction of narrative language as the future of literature: that there was no end to the possibilities, that linear text was worn out, finished. He told me about a story he was working on, full of enthusiasm for it. I couldn't follow what he was nattering on about.

I was much less certain about the subject. I realized that by writing and selling two experimental stories I must have some ability or facility with them. But I also knew that I had found both of them easier to write than the more formal attempts I had made earlier. In a sense, once I got the hang of the idiom, the story wrote itself. This chap was congratulating me on them. I liked that, naturally I liked that, but it deepened my inner doubts.

I asked him what he thought of the lyrics of John Lennon's 'I Am the Walrus' – not intended as a trick question, because I was genuinely puzzled by the song. It seemed to be about something, but there was a cleverness with words, a love of the *sound* of words, that made nonsense of meaning. At least to my ears: placing *expert* next to *textpert*, *choking* next to *smokers*, and so on. My friend said immediately: '"I Am the Walrus" is social comment.'

I couldn't see that. I thought about that assertion many times in the weeks that followed, because it seemed to me that although Lennon was far too interesting a lyricist to write nonsense for the sake of it, the sheer skill of the wordplay drew attention to itself. I knew the song well: I had played it a hundred times but I had never worked out its 'meaning' – and if it was commenting on society, then it was either doing so in such a profound way that the comment was beyond me, or Lennon was making fun of those who tried.

Years later, I read Ian MacDonald's brilliant exegesis on the words of this song in his book *Revolution in the Head*, in which he plausibly unravels Lennon's thoughts, influences and likely intentions at the time. MacDonald does not make out a case for social comment, though.

Hindsight allows us to unravel our own thoughts and intentions, even if they were not too clear to us at the time. Such was the case with me. I know I sensed that wordplay was something of a blind alley. I also heeded Michael Moorcock's gently worded advice, even though at the time I did tend to snort in a rebellious way. At least, not where he could hear me. I wanted to move on again.

Chance

(APRIL 1967)

Empty. A triangle of grass and tarmac.

Shepherds Bush at two in the morning. Deserted and damp. A trace of summer shower on drying paving stones. Dirt in a station booking office. An occasional lorry, and a row of parked cars.

And a couple, alone in the square.

Karen led him through several side streets, until they came to a road running roughly parallel with the main road. David walked beside her in silence. Earlier, as they had walked by the lake in the park, or in the pub or during the meal, they had talked incessantly.

The street was darker than the main road, but there was more activity. Many windows were lighted behind thin curtains. On a doorstep three long-haired girls huddled together smoking acrid foreign cigarettes. Two guys passed, talking excitedly in a foreign tongue. Loud music vibrated through a darkened open window. Three cars drove down the street, going much too fast.

He dropped his arm from around her back, and took her hand in his. As she responded he felt her fingers tighten.

This is Karen now, he thought. Twenty-six. For ten years he had carried an image of an unchanging sixteen-year-old girl, still gawky in her movements. The last time he'd seen her was in a dirty side street in Macclesfield, wearing a plastic mac and with her hair untidy and blown. He'd watched her eyes as he'd said goodbye. In his own awkwardness he'd felt nothing but a fierce infatuation for the girl he'd courted for three years.

Then the next day he'd boarded a train with his parents, and left for London.

On the next corner was a modern streetlamp, burning with a steady orange glow. Karen stopped beneath it.

'This my street,' she said. Looking at her eyes, David experienced a brief feeling of nostalgia. These were the eyes that had reflected his own emotions ten years before. Now they were happy, and David felt his old awkwardness return.

'Come on,' he said, almost brusquely. 'We're wasting time.'

She smiled. Her hand linked through his am. 'It takes two to do that,' she said.

David automatically memorized the name of the street: Sinclair Road, W.14.

Karen seemed to be leading, and this vaguely satisfied him. The tenderness of the afternoon and evening had set up a resistance in him towards sex. It all seemed too good and pure to destroy with physical satisfaction. Yet with the excitement of the day now replaced by a mutual tiredness, he was pleased that Karen was taking the initiative.

The street was long, and straight. Cars of every description were parked at its edge. Once, a Volkswagen brown in the sickly light from the street-lamps shot by with dazzling headlights.

Karen stopped suddenly by a doorway. She took her hand from David's arm, and reached in her bag.

'Look at me, Karen,' David said, still feeling the awkwardness. 'What is this going to do to us?'

'Do?'

'I mean ... Well, our relationship ...'

She pressed close to him and kissed his chin. The first time, he suddenly realized, since the shy kisses an hour after they'd met in the park. He touched her lips with his, and they kissed again.

Finally she broke away. 'We're not sixteen now, David. We'll get by.'

She felt again in her bag, and brought out a cheap plastic key fob holding several kinds of key. She inserted one in the lock, and opened the door.

She kissed him again. 'Now who's wasting time?' she said.

They climbed one flight of stairs, then another. At the top of the second flight, Karen pressed a switch and dim light from a low-watt bulb illuminated a dusty landing. The walls were a dirty yellow colour, contrasting with the brown of the doors. There were three of these; two together and one facing down the landing.

'We're safe,' Karen said. 'Jane's on holiday with her fiancé this week.' She pointed at the right-hand door. 'You go in, and I'll make some coffee. If you want the toilet, it's down there.'

Taking off the light-coloured anorak she'd alternately worn or carried during the day, she went into the kitchen. David opened the other door, fumbled around the doorpost for the light switch, and went in.

The floor was an untidy mess of magazines and papers. In opposite corners of the bedroom were two single beds. The one nearest the door was made up, but the other was untidily rumpled. By one wall was a rickety trestle table carrying a typewriter and a pile of books and papers. Beneath it were more books and magazines. A tape recorder lay on the chair, halfway through a tape. A line of cacti on the window shelf seemed dusty and dehydrated, lending an air of decayed heat to the room.

Oppressed by the atmosphere he loosened his tie, and took off his jacket.

He sat on the floor by the untidy bed, and leaned against its side. Idly he picked up one of the magazines and leafed through it. In the kitchen next door he could hear Karen moving about. Once, he heard a cup rattle in its saucer, and a tap filled a kettle.

After a while she came into the bedroom and sat on the bed he was leaning against.

For a while neither of them said anything. Then David leaned back and felt her legs behind him.

'What's the time?' he said in a voice which was intended to convey boredom, but managed to contain a noticeable streak of anxiety. While they'd sat there in silence, he'd been wrestling for something to say. It seemed that they'd managed to say all the important things during the day. He was feeling a barrier coming between them now that made conversation come unnaturally.

Perhaps it was the considerable time since they'd last met. Was it that they were now so intent on showing each other how much they'd grown up that they were losing the ability to communicate with each other?

Karen lay back on the bed and craned her neck to see the portable alarm clock on the bedside table. 'Ten to three,' she said, in a dull tone.

Sitting up again, she slid down the side of the unmade bed, and squatted beside David on the floor. She lay her head on his shoulder, and snuggled closer as his arm went around her. They kissed immediately; slowly at first and then with an increasing eagerness.

Presently they kneeled, and climbed on to the bed. Somewhere in the hall outside an electricity meter clicked, and the lights went out.

In the darkened front room overlooking Sinclair Road, the couple didn't notice.

Earlier that day, the blue Pullman from Conwell New Town had rolled slowly into Euston, and David Rierson alighted in London. The city lay dirty and hot. His unmarried brother had a flat in Paddington and though he had only the vaguest notion of how to find it, that was where he was heading.

He'd telegrammed his brother from Conwell the day before, warning him to expect him for an indefinite stay.

The taxi found the flat in the end. His brother had left a note pinned to the bathroom door, telling him to make himself at home, and that he'd be home by six. David dumped his two suitcases in the kitchen, and went in search of some lunch.

He took the Tube to Tottenham Court Road, and went to a small Greek café in Charlotte Street he'd visited the last time he was in London. Then, already feeling the benefit of the change of environment, he set out in the hot afternoon to see London.

He wandered first down Oxford Street, peering disinterestedly into the windows of the glossy fashion stores. Bored with the heat and the tired-looking women, he turned left and wandered for half an hour through the more shaded streets of Soho.

Eventually, he found himself crossing Mayfair, and came to Park Lane. Across the wide dual carriageway he saw the green of Hyde Park, and sprinted across the road. He walked for ten minutes across the grass, then found a tree and lay beneath it. It was cooler there, and the noise of the traffic was only just perceptible.

Afterwards he lay with Karen in the discomfort of the untidy bed. Where their skins pressed together he could feel the heat like pools of hot water. Karen's eyes were closed, and he kissed her face gently.

She smiled at him, and shook her long hair from across her face.

It was like an unexpected interlude in a piece of brassy modern jazz. The entire world seemed to have quietened. Neither of them made any serious attempt to speak.

It lasted for about ten minutes, then Karen pushed him firmly away from her, and rolled off the bed. She stood up in silhouette against the window.

'Christ, this place is untidy,' she said. She kicked at the pile of clothes they'd dropped on the floor.

David sat up in the bed. 'What's wrong with you?' he asked, irritated. 'Keep still for a while.'

Her profile against the thinly curtained window turned to look at him. He couldn't see her expression. She bent down, retrieved her slip and pulled it over her shoulders. Saying nothing, she left the room.

After half a minute the lights came on again, and he heard the bathroom door close behind her.

It was the dog he noticed first. A stupid, petty kind of dog – the sort that rich widows keep. It was running across the grass, yapping happily to itself in the sun. He ignored it, but when it ran up to him and started sniffing his legs he sat up and pushed it away.

It was then that he saw Karen. She was standing still, about twenty yards away, looking at him with an expression of surprise and delight. He looked back at her, in slow comprehension. Her face was familiar, but he couldn't place it at once. Then she smiled and walked towards him. He stood up awkwardly. Good God, he thought. It's Karen.

She said, 'Hello David. Fancy seeing you again.' He said, 'Is this your dog?' Then they both laughed. In a split second in a sunny park with traffic murmuring half a mile away, a ten-year gap was filled.

It was too good to be true. Even as they laughed at what had happened, David sensed that a snapped link in his life had repaired itself.

And so they talked, reliving the past and its memories of an adolescent infatuation. They sat down beneath the tree, forgetting for a moment the present that had brought them together.

Suspended in a bubble of the past, and oblivious to everything else.

Eventually, alone in the park before the shower sent them running to the lakeside café for shelter, they kissed.

It was unique.

By the time Karen returned from the bathroom, David had turned off the central light, and switched on the table lamp. He sat on the bed, and lit himself a cigarette. When Karen came back into the room, still wearing the slip, he lit her another cigarette and she sat on the bed beside him.

'We forgot the coffee,' she said.

'God, yes.'

'It didn't matter. The stove went off when the meter ran out. Do you still fancy a cup?'

He shook his head. 'It just seemed like a good idea at the time.'

'I'm out of sugar, anyway.'

Later, when they'd finished the cigarettes, they climbed back into the bed.

Unexpectedly, Karen put her arm around his neck, and snuggled up to him. 'David,' she said. 'Have you had any lovers before now?'

He laughed. 'Dozens,' he said.

'Be serious.'

'I wasn't happily married in the normal sense, although Irene was always there when I needed her. But I'd never really forgotten you.'

Karen laughed.

'It's easy to say that, I know. But it's quite true. During the bad times with Irene, I used to think about the past. And you. At one point I was even going to write to you.'

She was silent for a few moments. Then she moved a little closer to him. 'I wish you had,' she murmured.

After the rain they walked around the edge of the lake. Once or twice Karen looked worriedly at her watch. She clung to David's arm as they walked, and seemed to be extending the afternoon as long as she could.

Around five o'clock, she stopped. She had to take the dog back, she said. It was a part-time job, walking dogs for other people. And so they reluctantly moved, walking towards the Victoria Gate, and Bayswater beyond.

The dog's owner lived in a smart block of flats in the Bayswater Road. It took only a couple of minutes for Karen to disappear inside and return the dog. She made a short telephone call from the porter's lodge (a previous date, she said) and then they were free for the evening.

Hand in hand, they walked off in the direction of the West End.

As he lay in bed with her, David was thinking about his relationship with Karen. It wouldn't do, he thought, to enquire too far into her life. One of his best traits was a total honesty with himself, and he'd always known that his attitude towards women was possessive. It had had a lot to do with his crumbling marriage to Irene.

And particularly Karen, for whom he'd retained a subconscious feeling that made her his own. Even through marriage, she had remained a part of him.

But the Karen with whom he now laid was different from the image he'd carried around for ten years. Instead of the sober and predictable Karen he'd known in his teens, she was a mature and physically attractive woman whose character was liable to change erratically. Already in the course of the afternoon and evening he had seen her witty and amusing, naïve and ingenuous, cynical and worldly. At one point she had become depressed as he spoke of his breaking relationship with his wife.

So Karen had changed. So too had he in all probability.

Physically she was much the same. A little taller and plumper – and facially she was as he'd always remembered. But it wasn't superficial things that worried him.

He didn't want to enquire, but she was no stranger to sex. He knew he would be hurt if he found out too much. Just for the moment, he was glad to be reunited with her.

If there was more he had to know about her, he wanted it to come later.

They started the evening in a pub. There was nowhere they wanted to go. All they really wanted was freedom to talk, and try out their strangeness on each other. So they took the Tube to Leicester Square, and found a small pub in Gerrard Street. They sat for an hour, eking out a couple of beers.

It was here that David first told her he was married. Her reaction was one of surprise; she hadn't thought he would ever marry.

Jokingly he added, Unless it was to you.

Seriously, she regarded him then, and told him she'd often felt that way too. Now she became depressed, empathizing with him as he told her of how he could recognize the stages in the decay of his marriage.

And it was here that Karen told him about her engagement to a man at her office. She told him of her wedding plans and the house his parents were going to buy them, and the children she wanted. And she told him of her disappointment when the man broke it off two months before the wedding day.

David felt a strong note of jealousy as she told him this. He wondered, briefly, whether his telling her of his marriage had done the same to her. Perhaps that was why she had become depressed.

From the pub they moved on to an Italian restaurant next door. They both found the meal quite indigestible, experiencing a kind of suppressed excitement that took away all appetite.

Towards the end of the meal Karen became very quiet. She was looking at David across the table, and for the first time he was able to see her without the distraction of memory. Here eyes were the same, and her face and her hair. But she had matured and grown more attractive.

Across the table she held his hand. The waiter brought coffee and they sipped it slowly. The meal lifted their depression, and they started talking again.

Although he felt tired, David found himself staying stubbornly awake. Beside him, Karen lay with her eyes closed. Outside, the night was beginning to lighten.

He kissed her, and her eyes opened immediately.

'Asleep?'

She smiled. 'No. Just relaxing. It's been a long day.'

'Any regrets about this?'

'About what?'

David began to feel a little uncomfortable. 'You know. Sleeping together.'

'Of course not.' She sat up, and fished around for the cigarette packet. 'What's so strange about it?'

He didn't reply. He watched her as she lit her cigarette. Karen didn't smoke. What was she doing with that cigarette? He remembered the one time he'd persuaded her to try one, and how they'd laughed at her clumsiness. But Karen, the girl in bed with him, smoked expertly.

As she did so many other things.

They stayed at the restaurant as long as they dared, then moved on to another pub. This one was larger and more crowded. A pianist in the corner was crooning old-fashioned songs. Nobody seemed to be listening. A crowd of twenty-year olds, in deliberate opposition, were singing rugby-club songs with vigour.

They stuck it until ten-thirty, then moved on.

The evening was warm and still. A perfect July night. In spite of the traffic and the after-theatre crowds the evening was calm. They walked the length of the Embankment then, for want of something better to do, rode around the Circle Line from Charing Cross. The second time round they changed at Notting Hill, and took the first westbound Central Line train.

And came to Shepherds Bush.

He became aware of Karen's hand on his chest. With her left hand she was stroking his stomach.

He moved against her, and reached round with his arm. She lifted her head and kissed him. With his hand he felt inside her slip for her breasts. She responded immediately, bringing her left leg across his own. She kissed him again.

She had never let him touch her breasts. Once, in the circle of the Palace Cinema in Macclesfield he had tried, but she had frozen at once. The rest of the evening had passed in uncomfortable silence. And her attitude to any physical contact was reserved. He'd known her for six months before she'd allowed him to kiss her. Even their final farewell had been a formal and almost aloof ceremony. But this was all part of Karen's appeal.

She had changed. She was Karen, but no longer Karen.

Their lovemaking became more vigorous, and they rolled and struggled on the bed together. She welcomed him to her, and as they joined again David felt a violent mental withdrawal.

The Karen he had known no longer existed. The woman he was in bed with could be anybody. Karen was only a memory.

Sinclair Road, W.14. As they rounded the corner David memorized the name of the street automatically. Now Karen was leading him. He could almost feel the pull of her hand. The strangeness of the afternoon and evening, in the way in which it had been emotionally complete on an absolutely platonic basis, had set up an indefinable reaction against sex. Now that reaction seemed to have largely disappeared.

Come back for a coffee, she had said. And David felt he had appreciated the euphemism.

The street was long, and straight. Cars of every description were parked at its edge. Once, a Volkswagen brown in the sickly light from the streetlamps, shot by with dazzling headlights.

Karen stepped into a doorway.

'This is my flat,' she said. In the doorway it was dark, and she stood close to him. Suddenly she threw her arms around his neck, and kissed him eagerly. 'Oh David,' she breathed in his ear. 'It's been wonderful.'

For the first time they were totally alone. The street was quiet, and the closed darkness of the doorway was intimate and pleasant. A ten-year old image came to him, of the door to her parents' house in Macclesfield.

People change in ten years, but not much. This was still Karen, the girl who'd occupied his adolescent life. She still kissed the same. He tightened his arms around her shoulders and kissed her harder.

He opened the front of her anorak, and groped for her breasts.

Karen stiffened. 'Stop that,' she said in his ear.

He held her tighter with his am around her neck. He squeezed her breast again, determined.

With a sudden movement she pulled away from him, and stumbled back towards the door. '*Don't!*'

She fumbled her bag and found her key. Without turning she let herself in, and slammed the door. No lights came on. In a moment, he heard her slowly climb the stairs.

Alone in the street, David stood in confusion. Why had Karen never grown up?

A bedroom in Shepherds Bush. Dark, a little dirty. Cacti on the sill, thin curtains. A tape recorder, and a half-played tape. A brown, patterned carpet, rucked across the middle. Old linoleum.

Two beds, and a bedside table. And a lamp. Paperbacks on the floor. An ashtray on the table. A piece of crumpled cellophane. And a still-smouldering, half-smoked cigarette.

Two beds. One tidy, made up. The other rumpled, and.

Empty.

Chance - notes

Then:
'Chance' was an deliberate attempt to move away from the traditional subjects of SF. I was still interested in the feeling of 'otherness' that SF can induce, but by this time I had been reading outside the genre for a while and was waking up to a world of larger literary possibilities.

I became interested in finding some means of dealing with non-fantastic subjects in a different kind of way. 'Chance' was a reflection on how easy it is for a relationship between two young people to go wrong. In this sense the story is a precursor to some of my later novels, in particular *The Affirmation* and *The Glamour*.

The opening three paragraphs, avoiding verbs, are a reminder of 'Conjugation'. Perhaps fortunately, the rest of the story is told in conventional English.

Looking back, I now find myself irritated by these glimpses into old sexual hang-ups, worries about girls, and so on. The characters are said to be twenty-six but many of their actions, thoughts, etc., are more immature than that, or so they now seem. Maybe these are inadvertent insights into my own hang-ups of that period. But from the point of view of my writing, tackling these difficult subjects for the first time felt like a breakthrough that I found stimulating.

Now:
I believe this story is an interesting failure. It depends on the credibility of the two characters, which to some extent is well established. But their inner lives are immature, and most adult readers would not feel sympathy for the predicament described.

The style is clear and for the most part effective. The punctuation is mostly under control.

'Had set up a resistance in him towards sex.' – This is naïve. Surely after an enjoyable day with an old girlfriend he would be eagerly anticipating sex with her, not resisting the idea?

'A voice which was intended to convey boredom, but managed to contain a noticeable streak of anxiety.' – How would that sort of voice actually sound?

'Peering disinterestedly.' – 'Uninterestedly', or 'without interest.'

'David was thinking about his relationship with Karen. It wouldn't do, he thought, to enquire too far into her life.' – Why not? What taboos is he expecting to uncover? What this means is that David is unwilling to find things out about her life in the last ten years that he might find shocking.

'It [his possessive attitude] had had a lot to do with his crumbling marriage to Irene.' – This must mean instead that being possessive had had a lot to do with making his marriage go wrong?

'With whom he now laid.' – With whom he was now lying.

'Even their final farewell had been a formal and almost aloof ceremony.' – This is written so stiffly and awkwardly. These were teenagers, so formality and aloofness would not have been in their reactions to a difficult parting.

I had several goes at 'Chance', trying to get the story right. It went through several drafts, even, for a time, having its title changed to 'Second Chance'. I nipped that in the bud, since it seemed to open the way to endless redrafting, each successive version being given another ordinal. (The version here is the final working.) In the end I passed the story to Janet Freer, my newly discovered and proudly possessed literary agent, to see what she might do with it. I know she tried sending it to at least one magazine, but no sale materialized. It's fairly easy to see why.

The story represented another transition. The two previous stories had tried moving away from formal narrative prose, while dealing obliquely with fairly standard SF ideas. 'Chance' is for the most part entirely conventional in its prose, but it takes an unexpected, unreliable look at a relationship that exists in the real world. The story does not end as it might have seemed to be heading at the start, and I believe it is true to say that it is done without the use of a gimmick.

Ordinary life often works out in unanticipated ways. Most people are familiar with the idea of 'crossroads' in their lives, moments when a decision or an action was taken, and which later can be seen as either the right or wrong one – the well judged or the misguided.

Reminiscence is often based on this kind of thing: we daydream about old lovers, muse about houses that were never bought or lived in, remember jobs that were abandoned or never started, and so on. We sense that life might have been better *if only* ... or things might have turned out a lot worse, *if it hadn't been like that*.

This story in effect concentrates on one of those moments, the chance of a decision rightly or wrongly taken, expectations lost, knowledge never gained.

It was a liberating realization that fictional material could be so close to normal experience and yet take a sideways look at it, to act like an irregular form. It was another skill I could try to develop, a widening of the possibilities of what might be written.

The Interrogator

(JANUARY 1968)

Elias Wentik sat on the bunk in his cell and watched the pencil-beam of light crawl across the opposite wall. Periodically, he shivered; the temperature in the cell was not far above freezing.

The bunk was constructed of wooden planks, and lined with a thin covering of plastic foam. In the centre of the ceiling was an electric light, set in an breakable mould of hard smooth glass. (Once, in a moment of desperation, Wentik had tried to smash it to use the fragments on the veins in his wrists). On the wall furthest from the door was a massive loudspeaker through which two pieces of music were played simultaneously.

During the long nights his time was his own and, beyond the ordinary unpleasantness of the cell itself, he was left entirely undisturbed. Having no method of measuring time, Wentik had no idea of the length of the nights but they were certainly at least as long as twelve hours. He would sleep as long as he could, but he rarely succeeded in passing more than half' the time in this way.

The door was unlocked, but throughout the night there were always two guards on duty who permitted him to go no further than the toilet.

Wentik had dreamed, and watching the monotonous meandering of the light-beam he wondered what it had meant. Arstourd, his interrogator, had appeared before him in the uniform of a prisoner. In his hands he carried a rifle, and had fired it into the air as he spoke. Later, Wentik had walked alone on the shores of a small lake, watching the water drain away leaving its branch-strewn bottom exposed. Arstourd had appeared again, with a boat that was now useless, and he and Wentik had sat in it as if waiting for the lake to refill.

Footsteps disappeared down the corridor. The guards were

going off duty; another night was ended. Relieved, Wentik put his head round the door, and looked up and down the corridor. Sunlight outlined squares around the shuttered windows.

Now, for another twelve hours, he was free to wander through the prison as he pleased. The only restriction on his movement was that at least once during the day he had to see Arstourd in his room high in the upper floors of the prison, with the wide windows looking out across the plain. It was in this room that he was interrogated.

As he looked down the corridor, Wentik heard more footsteps approaching, and he ducked back into his cell. He sat on his bunk, and waited.

The door was kicked back, and it crashed against the wall. Two men in guards' uniforms marched in and hauled him to his feet. The sleeve of his shirt was ripped down and, to Wentik's sudden terror, a hypodermic needle thrust into his arm. Immediately, a consuming weakness overcame him. He slumped into the arms of the men. Nausea surged up through his body. Music roared in a two-part disharmony around the cell, and the light in the ceiling began to flash on and off. He vomited on to the floor, watching the sickly red liquid of his last meal flow under the bunk.

The men dragged him round, and pulled him towards the door. One of the guards tramped on his unshod foot, and his face curled with agony.

At the end of the corridor, and after descending two flights of rough stone steps, they came to a light wooden door which in the past had always been locked. One of the guards rattled a small key-ring, and unlocked it. The other booted it open, and Wentik was thrown bodily through. He stumbled forward, and collapsed into a heap on the soft grass.

The sunshine was blinding.

'Stand up, Wentik. I have some questions to ask you.'

Wentik looked up at his interrogator. It was Arstourd, his face invisible, outlined by a corona of sunlight. Wentik's eyes, weakened by the drug, watered, and he was forced to blink. He looked down at the grass. A tiny insect was crawling tirelessly through the stalks, making erratic progress. Wentik stared at it.

In front of him, Arstourd turned to a group of white-coated men and beckoned. Two of them started across the lawn towards him, and Arstourd walked away from his prisoner.

Wentik sprawled on the grass and looked across the lawn. Arstourd was walking away from him and two men in Arstourd was walking away from two men in white Arstourd was walking towards him in two white men in Arstourd coats was walking to the insect was erratic walking down grass to the Arstourd white coat was two men was white Arstourd sun behind two men in white coats were walking towards him.

Wentik blinked.

It was a small square of lawn, surrounded by tall, green trees. The sky was a deep blue and the sun was hot in the sky. Winged squirrels soared screaming from one tree to another and a cloud of insects hovered beneath a branch of the largest tree. In the centre of the lawn was a large wooden table with two chairs standing on opposite sides.

Where was he? He looked behind him, saw a high concrete wall. The door through which he'd been thrown was closed. Beside it was a small, dust-covered window, from which stared the faces of the two guards.

Wentik tried to stand, rolled over on to his back. His head fell backwards, and banged painfully on the soft earth. He stretched his neck, so he was looking fully into the sun. Saw the two white-coated men halfway across the lawn towards him. Why were they walking upside down? Why was a table glued to a ceiling of grass with Arstourd sitting at it – and the two men crawled like insects across the grass and grabbed his arms. Helplessly, he allowed them to drag him to the table.

The two men (scientists, Wentik guessed) threw him into the other seat, a cane chair which sagged uncomfortably under his weight. He sprawled across the table, feeling the heat of the sun on his exposed neck. The men left him on the table, and walked back to the others. One of the men who'd not moved said something to one of the two who had. All the scientists laughed.

From the angle at which his head was lying, Wentik could see the men clearly. His eyes were watering no longer, growing accustomed to the brilliance of the sun. The scientists were standing in the shade of one of the trees and several of them sipped at tall drinks. One of the men had a stethoscope around his neck, and about five of them carried clipboards.

Nobody moved.

At the back of the garden was the high concrete wall. From where he lay, Wentik could not easily see it. He rolled his head over. A hundred blank and dust-covered windows stared down at him.

Wentik sat up and lolled back in the chair, nearly causing it to collapse backwards. He re-surveyed the scene. The sun was shining, and it was too hot. There were a lot of insects everywhere and the screaming of the squirrels was unpleasant. Across the table sat Arstourd.

Reason returned to Wentik, with a chill that momentarily took away the heat of the sun. He was still a prisoner, and he was going to be interrogated. It was the Method, after all. (A subtle diversion to disorient him?) Perhaps he was forming too solid a block against the questioning.

Arstourd said, 'Tell me your name, Wentik.'

Staring blandly, he smiled at his prisoner. Wentik looked across the table, his eyes focusing properly for perhaps the first time. Arstourd was in plain grey uniform. Both of his hands were resting on the top of the table. His smile broadened, and a sense of horror struck Wentik.

There were three hands on the table. And Arstourd had only two.

He stared and Arstourd's smile grew wider and the scientists laughed and a squirrel screamed.

A hand was growing from the centre of the table. Not resting there, like Arstourd's, but *growing*. Wentik could see where it joined the smooth wood.

It was pointing at him.

'Your name, Wentik. Give me your name.'

High in the sky, somewhere far above the square of grass, a jet aircraft roared. Behind Arstourd's head, outside the garden and nearly on the horizon, a small hill rose above the level of the plain. On its summit Wentik could see a metal mast. The effects of the drug were wearing off fast – Wentik began to feel almost normal.

He looked again at the hand growing from the centre of the table. It was built perfectly, like a Greek carving in skin and flesh. It was the normal size of a man's hand, pale in the sunlight, but not bloodless. Tiny blond hairs grew on its back, refracting the sunlight. About three inches of wrist were visible before the arm disappeared into the table-top, fusing into the grainy, dark-stained wood. Incredibly, the hand started to drum its fingers, like those of a man kept waiting for an appointment.

'Your name!'

He took a breath. 'My name is Elias Wentik.'

The hand stopped its drumming, and relaxed on the table. It rested motionlessly as if waiting.

'What is your crime?'

'I –' He hesitated, and thought to himself, *But there is no crime. I'm innocent* – The hand was pointing at him, accusing him.

'I have not committed any crimes.' The hand remained steady.

Arstourd slammed his own right hand against the table-top, and started to rise. 'No crimes, Wentik? Your guilt is beyond doubt, yet you have committed no crimes! Now the truth!'

In the centre of the table, the rooted hand started stabbing in the air towards him. Wentik watched it, fascinated.

Sitting down again, Arstourd said, 'You see, I have no doubt of your guilt. All I require is an admission of your crime.'

Wentik nodded.

The hand was fascinating him. It seemed to act entirely of its own will, disconnected from any apparent external control. It was one hell of a trick.

Wentik pushed his chair backwards, and dropped to his hands and knees. The grass was warm to his hands, bringing the recollection of the many summers of his youth when he'd stretched for hours on the College lawns with his wife. The memory entered and left his awareness in a flash; it was part of a world he had now lost.

He crawled beneath the table, and looked up at the underside of the top surface. It was completely plain, giving no clue to the mechanism of the hand. Arstourd's legs, protruding under the table, were wide apart and clad in badly-fitting army trousers. Up near the man's crotch Wentik could see a tiny gap in the seam, pulled apart by the strain of the man's posture. He crawled out again, and stood behind Arstourd. The man was motionless, scarcely seeming even to breathe. On the table the hand continued to stab the air in the direction of his empty seat.

The scientists were watching him carefully. Two of them were writing quickly on their clipboards, and another was holding some kind of a watch.

Experimentally, Wentik walked directly away from them, parallel to the high wall of the building.

At the edge of the grass there was a narrow strip of bare soil, then the line of trees. As he walked beneath two of the large beeches, Wentik noticed that he had disturbed a colony of ants. As he passed, thousands of the tiny insects ran aimlessly about.

Beyond the trees there was a vast field of stubble, stretching as far as he could see. Clear of the shade from the trees he was immediately aware of the heat from the sun. There was no shade anywhere, and as he stepped carefully between the prickly clumps of stubble (he was still unshod) he accepted that there would be no escape for him across the endless plain. He squatted on his haunches, facing back towards the lawn. The scientists had left the comfort of the shade and were walking slowly towards him across the stubble.

To Wentik, they appeared rather bored by what was going on.

Later, back in his cell, Wentik reviewed what had happened and thought again about the events leading up to his imprisonment.

Arstourd was the key to everything. He'd known the man for some time, when he'd come to the Advanced Technique Concentration where Wentik was leading the research into sub-neutronic radiation. Out there on the Antarctic ice-cap, a thousand miles from civilization, the indignities caused by Arstourd's early interrogations had felt removed from reality and were only a part of the general difficulty of life in the sub-zero conditions.

Flying back to the city, a month later, Arstourd had relaxed for the first and only time in Wentik's presence, and had told him a series of obscure anecdotes about life in the army. Wentik noticed, during the telling of one of the tales, how Arstourd's tiny eyes had gleamed with agitation.

'... but he lasted twelve months, and had to be released!' the story finished, and Arstourd doubled across his seat with mirth. Politely, Wentik smiled.

His ordeal in the jail started slowly enough. He was given the freedom of the building from the start, and wandered around it lethargically. His early impressions of it were that it was a form of elaborate maze. On no two days were the same doors left open. His route through the bleak building was always controlled by the combination of those unlocked. One corridor was always open to him, and its windows overlooked the yard at the rear of the building. Here, a gang of fifteen men laboured constantly to erect a working windmill, and in his early days at the jail Wentik had spent long hours gazing across the tiny space, quietly mocking them for their unguided and uncoordinated efforts. Later, immoveable blinds were screwed across the windows the length of the corridor, and this small pleasure was taken away from him.

Gradually, his tiny privileges were restricted, and the only movement he was allowed was along the corridor that connected the cells and up to the room where he was normally interrogated.

He was the only prisoner in the block, but sometimes he could hear shouting voices in the distance. He assumed at first that the voices came from the labourers, but he was told that the windmill had been abandoned and the navvies had left. Meals were collected by him from the crude kitchen in the basement, but soon he was restricted to the corridor and the food was brought to him.

Two months after he arrived at the jail, and was beginning to accept the featureless routine of aimless exercise along the corridor and the interminable and inconclusive interrogation sessions with Arstourd, two guards came for him and dragged him down to a wooden shack erected some three hundred metres from the main building. Here, he was thrown through the door and left to wander unguided through an endless maze built of thin wooden sheets, while outside the guards fired blank cartridges into the air.

On another occasion he was given a metal pole and a face shield, and told to explode buried landmines in a plot of ground one hundred metres square. Five mines were buried in the soil, and he had to destroy them all. Six hours later, with four of the mines destroyed (each time with an explosion that damaged his nerves more than his body) they called off the search, telling him that the fifth mine did not exist.

With the tedium of the interrogation broken in this way, Wentik passed three more slow months.

His interrogator was always Arstourd, and he was always asked the same questions. His name. His purpose. His employers. His crimes – always his crimes. Arstourd was like a machine; prowling about the room, dressed in the stiff grey uniform that gave no clue to his rank, putting his questions in his high-pitched, querulous voice.

And the room was always the same, in the wing overlooking the barren plain.

As often happened, when Wentik awoke he discovered his cell door was unlocked. He stepped out into the corridor, and for twenty minutes roamed through the empty jail building. As he walked he found most of the catches on the doors were locked, except those that led down in the direction of the lawn. He caught faint snatches of a piano concerto as he wandered, played softly and with feeling at a level just above the point of inaudibility. Nowhere in the building could he get near enough to it to identify it, yet its melody was constantly on the fringes of recognition.

Finally, he admitted to himself that the only way he could walk was down to the lawn.

Arstourd was sitting at the table again, his face as expressionless as ever.

'Sit down, Wentik,' he said as soon as he saw him.

Wentik walked cautiously to the table, noting that the hand still grew from its centre. It was motionless, its fingers resting limply on the surface of the table.

As he reached the table, Wentik looked around the lawn. He and Arstourd were alone. There was no sign of the scientists in their white coats.

The day before, the small garden had held something of the aspect of a dream and Wentik, before he sat at the table, looked around it, attempting to view it more clearly. Everything was as before. The close-cropped lawn; the wall of the jail forming one side and the beech trees forming three sides of the garden; the blank undulating plain stretching to the horizon; the shack they'd taken him to the first time; and near it the square of open soil where they said they'd buried five landmines.

And in the centre of the table was the hand.

Wentik sat down. He stared at the hand and thought, *My name is Clive Arstourd.* The hand pointed at him. He thought again, *I am a free man.* The hand was steady. *I am a prisoner, and my name is Elias Wentik.* The hand slackened, and returned to its former position.

So, to some degree it could be controlled.

Arstourd was watching him. Perhaps he could be similarly controlled.

'Who employs you, Wentik?'

Wentik watched the hand. He tried, *I am a government scientist*, and it didn't tremble. 'I *I* am *am* a *a* civilian *scientist*,' he said, carefully controlling his thoughts.

Arstourd was also watching the hand. 'What were you doing at the Concentration?'

'I *I* was *was* being *experimenting* used *with* as *an* a *isotope* human *that* subject *could* in *wipe* the *out* radiation *a* experiments *continent*,' Wentik replied, acutely conscious that he could not keep this up for long. The expression on Arstourd's face was one of absorption.

'What nationality are you?' he said.

'American *American*.'

'Who am I?'

'You are my interrogator.'

The hand snapped into rigidity, pointing straight at him. Arstourd stood up and walked away, and from behind the beech trees fringing the lawn stepped the scientists.

Suddenly amused, Elias Wentik began to laugh, and walked back unassisted to his cell.

What he would like was an hour alone with the hand. It was evident that he could manipulate it in a way Arstourd had not anticipated he could. Think a deliberate lie, and the hand pointed at him. Think the truth and say a lie, and it stayed motionless. Say a lie with equal deliberation, and the hand pointed at him.

It wasn't enough just to believe in the answer – his answer to the last question was an expression of what he honestly believed. Yet the hand had accused him of a lie. Perhaps it depended also on the way Arstourd *expected* him to answer.

This in itself raised a query. Why was Arstourd there at all if the hand's reaction was in any way independent?

The next time he sat at the table, Wentik replied with nothing but what he thought was the truth. The questions were the same as always, and he answered them with a bland indifference to the outcome of his replies. Arstourd's reaction was passive and disinterested. Halfway through the questioning the scientists, who this time had been sitting in canvas chairs in the shade of the trees, wandered off towards the shack.

Ignoring Arstourd, Wentik too left the lawn and walked back to his cell. As he reached the wooden door he turned and looked back. Arstourd had slumped across the table, and the hand was lying flaccid.

At the next interrogation, he started to tell nothing but contradictory rubbish. Arstourd became agitated in the extreme; standing on his side of the table, clutching its edge and screaming the same questions over and over. The hand became white with rigidity.

Thus equipped with information about the hand, Wentik returned to his cell and slept restfully for the first time since he'd been at the jail.

Three days later, strolling down the corridor on his way to the garden, Wentik noticed the windows overlooking the courtyard had been unshuttered. The windmill was as he had last seen it, in a half-erected state. As he watched, a gang of men carrying ropes and tackle entered the yard and looked appraisingly up at the mill.

When he reached the lawn, Wentik did not go straight to the table. Instead he walked around the perimeter of the grass until he came to where the scientists were standing. They seemed a little startled that he should go up to them directly.

Wentik approached the nearest, a youngish man with black hair greased down over his skull. He looked apprehensively at Wentik.

'Who are you?' Wentik said.

'Me? I'm Johns. Derek Johns.' He pointed at the others. 'And that's Wilkes, and that's Mesker, and Wallis and ...'

Wentik moved on, around and behind the men. Idly, he picked up one of the clipboards lying on the ground. The sheet was divided into two broad margins, headed *Reactive* and *Progressive*. In both columns were noted several tiny equations, like absent-minded scribble doodled in a preoccupied moment. At the bottom, in the *Progressive* column someone had written:

Arstourd
Wentik
Arstourd

The last name was heavily underlined.

The scientist whose name was Johns, said suddenly, 'Are you breaking him down?'

Wentik, still puzzling over the meaning of the notes, said abstractedly, 'Who? Arstourd?'

'Of course. Who else is there?'

Not getting any sense from this Wentik moved away from the group of scientists towards a corner of the lawn. He sat down in the shelter of one of the beech trees, and studied the hieroglyphics on the clipboard. Johns had followed him over, and squatted beside him. Above their heads a squirrel suddenly leaped across the lawn, startling them both. Its scream hovered in the confined space.

'Look,' Johns said, 'I can get this over for you quickly if you want. Do you know how long you've been here?'

'No. I began to lose sense of time when the windows in the corridor were boarded up.'

'It's six months.'

Wentik looked across the lawn at the table, where Arstourd was still sitting. The man was gazing blankly at the hand growing from its centre.

'What does Arstourd hope to gain from the questioning? Over and over, they're the same questions. It no longer even matters how I answer them.'

Johns glanced at him shrewdly. 'Maybe that's the fault of the questioner rather than the questions.'

'Meaning ...?'

The scientist stood up and turned away. 'That's for you to discover.'

Wentik said, 'For me? I don't understand.'

Johns turned back to him. 'What does Arstourd mean to you? What are your feelings towards him?'

'I despise him,' Wentik said. 'He's inhuman. That a man could question another for so long is inconceivable. I've often wondered whether or not he's human.'

Johns walked away, leaving Wentik holding the clipboard. He looked again at it, but could get no sense from it. Finally, he dropped it on the soil and looked across at the group of scientists. Johns had rejoined them and they were watching him casually, almost as if he were of secondary importance to something which had yet to happen.

Arstourd sat alone at his table, in the centre of the lawn.

Patiently, Wentik sat beneath his tree waiting to see what would happen. The sun was hot again, causing the distant horizon to waver. Nobody moved, though occasionally he would see someone pass a window in the jail block. The silence was incredibly deep, broken only once by a jet aircraft crossing the sky at great height and speed.

On a sudden impulse, Wentik jumped up and sprinted across the lawn towards the jail. A face had moved past the window near the light wooden door. He kicked it open, and found a surprised guard walking slowly down the corridor. He leaped on to the guard's back, and crooked his arm in a strangling hold around the man's throat. The guard threw up his arms, but Wentik had him in an unbreakable hold. He dragged him to the floor.

Satisfied that the man could not escape, Wentik relaxed his grip slightly so he could speak.

'What's your name?' he said into the man's ear.

'Adams, sir. Don't grip me like that. I can't breathe.'

'OK. But I want information. Where the hell is this?'

The guard struggled slightly, but Wentik maintained his hold. 'It's not where this is, it's when.'

'What do you mean? Be specific.' He tightened his hold again, very slightly.

The man wriggled again, then said, 'We're in the Allto District, and –'

Wentik stopped listening. He knew enough. The Allto District was that area of the Brazilian Matto Grosso where time was a concept abstract and inessential, and the terrain of the country bore no similarity to the rest of the forest. There was no way of estimating its real place or presence: to walk in the Allto District was to leave the world of the present and find a future world. Men had estimated its presence as being anywhere between a hundred and a thousand years in the future. No one lived there, yet strange aircraft were to be seen passing high overhead. An ideal place for a jail: no one who had entered was known to leave.

When there is no escape from a jail, who are the imprisoners and who are the imprisoned?

Wentik released the guard, who scuttled away fingering his throat. More sure of himself, Wentik returned to the bright sunlight of the lawn.

Arstourd was sitting at the table as before. He looked up as Wentik approached. 'Sit down, Wentik,' he said.

Instead, Wentik continued to walk around the table. In the centre the hand rested idly, aimed in the general direction of the empty chair. Looking for a moment at the trees, he noticed that the scientists were alert, as if his movements were once again of major interest. Suddenly, Wentik seized the table and swivelled it round so that the hand pointed at Arstourd.

'Why am I here, Arstourd? Tell me!' He jumped up in front of the man, waved a threatening fist. In the centre of the table the hand was pointing.

Arstourd fell backwards from his chair, and rolled on the grass. He tried to squirm away but Wentik, still holding the table, turned it again so the aim of the hand followed the man. It began to stab the air.

Arstourd said, shouting, 'Don't point that at me!'

He crawled away towards the group of scientists. Wentik dropped the table, and ran after him. He caught him, and dragged him to his feet.

'Why have you been interrogating me?' he shouted at the man.

Arstourd stared. at him bleakly. 'But – But it's the other way round. Leave me alone! I've shared your guilt long enough.'

He pulled himself free of Wentik's grip and ran through the group of scientists and across the plain towards the shack. Reaching its outer door, he disappeared inside.

Johns, the scientist, said to Wentik, 'I take it you understand now?'

'Not really,' Wentik replied. 'In, fact, I'm at rather more of a loss.'

Johns walked over to the table and righted it. The hand in its centre was still stabbing blindly. 'It's this device that's crucial.' He ran his fingers along the edge of the table, hesitated over a particular place, and the hand relaxed again. 'While Arstourd was in control of himself and the hand, he felt you could carry all the blame.'

Wentik said, 'But why the blame? What have I done?'

'It's not what you've actually done. More what you were likely to do. The work at the Concentration ...'

'That was pure research. I had no idea what the outcome would be.'

'Maybe not. But we know the device that your work would ultimately produce. At least, we do now. He gestured vaguely at the surrounding plain, simmering in the heat from a sun unknown years into the future.

'And Arstourd?'

'That's our next problem. You were our first. We used Arstourd partly as a blind to our real intentions –'

'Which were?'

'– and partly because somewhere he has a genuine share of the guilt. It was he that warned us of the outcome of your work.'

Wentik noticed the rest of the scientists had taken off their white laboratory coats, and were walking slowly across the plain towards the shack.

He said, 'But what's the purpose of this?'

Johns said, enigmatically, 'I'll answer that as soon as I can.

Now let's find what we can from Arstourd.'

He walked away from Wentik towards the trees, taking off his white coat as he walked. Wentik followed him, noticing that underneath the coat Johns was wearing the uniform of the guards. He went to the pile of discarded coats, and picked one up.

'May I put this on?' hc called to Johns.

There was no reply, so he pulled it across his shoulders and slipped his arms down the sleeves. On the ground he found a discarded clipboard, and he picked that up too. The paper was blank.

He sat in the shade of the trees for an hour, watching the implacable face of the jail. There was no movement that he could detect, though from time to time he heard banging noises from the other side; the labourers in the yard, he guessed, working on their infernal windmill.

At the end of the hour the men standing around the shack roared their delight, and blank cartridges rattled into the air. Every now and then a man would scream, his voice muffled by the thin walls of the shack.

Much later, in the undiminishing heat of the long afternoon, Wentik found a rifle and some blank ammunition by one of the trees and strolled across the plain to the others at the shack.

The Interrogator - notes

Then:

There is a gap of several months between 'The Interrogator' and the story that preceded it. Not long after completing 'Chance' I pulled up roots and moved away from my parents' house in Essex. I went to live in a rented flat in Chelsea, in south-west London. I was 23 and it was 1967, the summer of love. I happened to be living almost at the epicentre of what the Americans called 'swinging London'. My flatmates were three young men of approximately my own age.

I was restless and unhappy in my job, getting away with my incompetent accountancy by the skin of my teeth in a greetings-card manufacturer's office in north London. (I had been fired from my job in the professional wing of accountancy the year before. The articles that protected me had finally expired, and without them out I went. The partners of WS&L made a correct and timely decision. I have never felt able to thank them enough.) Getting up to north London was a tiresome daily commute from Chelsea, so not long after the move I found a job with a mail-order publisher in Wandsworth, a short bus-ride or a long walk from where I lived.

There in a firm called Heron Books I became the Book Production Manager, but the title was better than the job. It involved hours of arithmetic trying to predict how many copies of various titles would need to be printed, and when by. This was a calculation which could have been completed in nano-seconds if only computers had been available at the time.

The only notable thing about the job, I now realize, is that I shared an office suite with a young man who had immense feet and a pleasant West Country burr, who was heavily into body-building, and who did a spot of acting on the side. His name was Dave Prowse, and not long after this he was to play Julian in Stanley Kubrick's film *A Clockwork Orange*, and Darth Vader in the *Star Wars* films.

Every evening, and every weekend, I set up my typewriter on a wobbly table in the apartment and wrote and wrote and wrote. Outside in the world, most people of my age were getting stoned for the first time, or dressing in flamboyant clothes, or deafening themselves with rock music, or discovering the joys of what was called even then an alternative lifestyle.

All this passed me by – I was focused on only one thing, and that was to succeed as a writer. Perhaps it sounds obsessive, self-denying, unworldly, but I didn't think like that. Because I was having to look after my own domestic life for the first time, and because I had the full-time job, I felt irreproachably integrated into mundane reality. The book world in general, and writing in particular, were the only things that completely interested me. I had already turned up some small successes, and I wanted to build on them.

Janet Freer, my agent, seemed to have faith in me, and she often telephoned with suggestions about magazines or book publishers who were looking for commercial material. That wasn't exactly the work I wanted to do, but I reckoned that having a go at it would be useful practice. During that summer of 1967 I therefore wrote a handful of the commercial short-short stories I mentioned earlier. The quality of the results was mixed, but the stories were published and they made me some pocket money. I rationalized the time spent on them in terms of learning more about the craft of writing.

However, they were obviously not what I wanted to write, and between times I started a draft of what I intended would be my first novel. I found it awfully hard going, but I persevered with a steady output of two pages an evening. After about a month I had some fifty pages of so-so draft, but it came to a halt. Six years later the idea for that story I was writing was to become my third novel, *Inverted World*, but in 1967 a work of such scale was clearly beyond me. After fifty mediocre pages I admitted defeat. I gave it up and destroyed what I had written. Nothing was lost – the stuff was no good.

I lowered my sights and began to think again about a series of images that had been haunting me for some time.

In 1966 I had seen the Hungarian film, *Szegénylegények,* better known in the UK under the title *The Round-Up* (I found that easier to remember), directed by Miklós Jancsó. The monochrome images of the concentration camp on the Puszta plains of Hungary, with cruel and unusual punishments meted out in an attempt to break the prisoners' will, had left a lasting impression on me. As the ideas of 'The Interrogator' started taking shape, locating an isolated jail in the centre of a featureless plain became irresistible.

This story shows a further move away from the traditional

materials of science fiction, and the beginning of the process by which I was at last finding my own voice as a writer. The adolescent attractions of SF were an increasing distance behind me, although I was still drawn to the fantastic metaphor as a way of telling an unusual story.

I had recently discovered the cool, terrifying novels of Jerzy Kosinski, I admired the casual impressionism of Nicholas Mosley, I liked the elegantly controlled emotionalism of Graham Greene. Stylistically, the matter-of-fact English of George Orwell was a lure I found irresistible. All these writers had produced work that was to my mind uncategorizable and uncopyable, but like J. G. Ballard a few years earlier they suggested ways forward that I might be able to take for myself.

'The Interrogator' was intended to be a kind of mix between the images of the Jancsó film and the cerebral intensity of Ballard's short stories. There are a few nods to the new wave, but not many – by the time I wrote 'The Interrogator' I had almost entirely negative feelings about the movement. I believed it had become another kind of literary idiom, almost an establishment, with insiders and grudges and factions. I was responding to the constant instinct to go my own way, wherever that might be.

I submitted 'The Interrogator' to E. J. ('Ted') Carnell, but he rejected it. Because he made some encouraging comments, and urged me to consider rewriting and perhaps expanding the story, I never showed it to any other editor. One of the improvements Ted Carnell suggested was that I should change Arstourd's name, because it sounded like 'arse-turd.' In later versions, Mr Arstourd therefore became Mr Astourde.

What happened after I rewrote the story is described in the Afterword.

> *Now:*
> At last the language and sentence structure are more or less under control. The story is cool and disturbing, mystifying, intriguing. The images are memorably clean. There is an

impression of confidence to much of the story. On the other hand ...

It is also cryptic and obscure – we are not given adequate motives for either of the two main characters. Wentik seems to accept his imprisonment without complaint, and what on Earth is Arstourd up to? And how many other people are present at the jail? Why are there no women? How do they get food or water, what do all those guards and scientists actually do when the half-hour of interrogation each day has been completed? Don't any of these people have families who are wondering where they have gone? The overall situation is maddeningly vague.

The dialogue with Derek Johns. He seems about to spill the beans, but changes the subject suddenly. The conversation with him becomes obscure and annoying. The crypticism is transparent here – it feels as if the writer is deliberately concealing information.

The dream sequence is acceptably short, but the story would be better without it. The entire story has a dreamlike quality, and Wentik's reported dream is a case of nervous over-egging.

'Another night was ended.' – Why not 'had ended'?

'The two men (scientists, Wentik guessed).' – This paranoia about scientists seems unfounded. This group of men is used as a sort of Fellini-like chorus.

'And Arstourd had only two.' – (Hands, that is.) A statement of the totally obvious, the one moment when the writer's confidence in the images seems to waver.

'Wentik replied, acutely conscious that he could not keep this up for long.' – In view of what Wentik had just been quoted as saying, this was something of an understatement.

'Arstourd's reaction was passive and *disinterested*.' – Since 1968 I have been pedantic about the correct usage of this invaluable word.

'Wentik stopped listening. He knew enough. The Allto District was that area of the Brazilian Matto Grosso where time was a concept abstract and inessential, and the terrain of the country bore no similarity to the rest of the forest.' – I can't hope to explain this, other than to say it was clearly a belated attempt to come up with some sort of logical background. The attempt failed.

Afterword

The end of the period covered by this book is marked by 'The Interrogator'. As noted above, it was rejected in a constructive way by E. J. Carnell, and the implied promise that he would look favourably on a re-submission concentrated my mind wonderfully.

Ted Carnell had edited *New Worlds* for many years before Michael Moorcock took over – he had been one of the people instrumental in setting up the monthly magazine not long after the end of World War 2. Much of the material in the Carnell-edited *New Worlds* was pedestrian and repetitive, with an emphasis on Earthmen landing on puzzling alien planets, where eventually they would solve, or sometimes be destroyed by, whatever the secret happened to be. You had only to read two or three of these stories to get the general idea and feel that reading any more of them was not urgent. More and more of them was what you found, especially in the later issues Carnell published, and I have always believed that this dire and dull story format did more to kill that version of the magazine than anything else.

I have also always believed that Ted Carnell had no particular or personal liking for planetary exploration teams and their ilk, but that he was sent them in increasing numbers by writers who believed that this was the sort of thing that he would buy.

The worst of science fiction, the stuff by which the stick-in-the-muds are so eager to judge the whole genre, has always been based on slavish imitation of what is perceived by unambitious writers to be the market. Only those writers who strike out on their own leave any kind of mark.

The evidence in defence of Ted Carnell is the fact that he had published most of the earliest stories by Brian Aldiss and J. G. Ballard. These were the two SF writers I most admired, and for a long time *New Worlds* was the only place where you could find their current work. For being able to read the work of these two alone I was prepared to forgive and forget the planetary stories. Carnell's loyalty to these two marvellous writers made him the one editor I wanted to sell stories to.

However, the Carnell era at *New Worlds* ended just about the same time as I got going. Not long afterwards, he began producing a quarterly series of SF anthologies for Corgi Books, called *New Writings in SF*. I sent him a couple of my earlier stories, but he always rejected them swiftly and politely. 'The Interrogator' was the first story of mine to gain his interest. The version rejected by him is the one published here.

I revised the story and sent it back to Carnell in April 1968. I had taken most of his comments seriously, doubled the length to 10,000 words, and in general made it much better. He bought it by return of post, and it was published in *New Writings in SF - 15*. (This, incidentally, was the first time my work had appeared in book form, as *NWiSF* was published in both paperback and hardback.)

Later in the year I wrote a 'sequel' to the story, called 'The Maze', also 10,000 words in length. To my chagrin, Ted Carnell rejected it with the same swiftness and courtesy as before.

Although 'The Maze' was actually not too bad, it was a direct follow-on from the earlier story. Carnell explained that had he been publishing a regular magazine he could have got away with printing a sequential story of that sort, but books were more of a stand-alone matter. I took his point, even though I was disappointed. I was also worried about money. I had just given up my job and was launching myself as a freelance writer, and had rather been relying on seeing 'The Maze' in print. It represented £40 I was foolishly counting on, and in its day the loss of it, or more accurately the non-receipt, presented me with a serious practical problem of survival.

Twenty thousand words of fiction represented a sustained effort, so once I had rallied after Ted Carnell's rejection I bundled the two long stories together and sent them to the publishers Victor Gollancz. I hoped they might commission me to write a novel based on them. They did not. No hard feelings. I sent the stuff to Charles Monteith at Faber & Faber instead, and he bought it. It felt like a miracle to me when he did.

The story of Wentik and Astourde became the basis of my first novel, *Indoctrinaire*, which Faber published in the summer of 1970. They paid me an advance of £150, coincidentally the same as my first pitiful salary as a hopeless accountancy trainee ten years before. The comparison is slightly false, because I had received my minuscule salary in weekly handouts, and the Faber advance was in three instalments and spread over eighteen months. However, to sell my first novel, unwritten and in outline only, to a major publisher like Faber was a real breakthrough, and I counted my lucky stars.

I told Charles I was pleased and did not reveal what a lousy accountant I had been. I was hoping not to be a lousy writer, and I did not want him to draw parallels. In reality, Charles Monteith's confidence in me launched me as a writer, and I have not had to do an honest job since.

For those who take an interest in such things, what was 'The Interrogator' became Chapters One to Six in the novel, and 'The Maze' became Chapters Seven to Ten.

All writers have to start somewhere, and every story of a writer's early career is necessarily different. My own growth from incompetent beginner to adequate learner, and then from there to being professionally published and soon after that to becoming a full-time writer, was comparatively brief – five years from start to finish, give or take a few weeks. The words with which I did that are here in this book, laid out for all to see.

These stories are not intended to explain or excuse or brag about what I did. They are simply to encourage others, who might have now the same objective as I had then.

Printed in the United Kingdom
by Lightning Source UK Ltd.
133460UK00002B/1-87/P

9 780955 973543